BREAKING HEARTS

DELTA FORCE STRONG BOOK #5

ELLE JAMES

TWISTED PAGE INC

BREAKING HEARTS

DELTA FORCE STRONG BOOK #5

New York Times & USA Today
Bestselling Author

ELLE JAMES

ISBN-13: (Ebook edition) 978-1-62695-333-8

ISBN-13: (Paperback edition) 978-1-62695-334-5

Dedicated to my daughters who share my love of reading.
You're beautiful and I love you both so very much.
Elle James

AUTHOR'S NOTE

Enjoy other military books by Elle James

Delta Force Strong

Ivy's Delta (Delta Force 3 Crossover)

Breaking Silence (#1)

Breaking Rules (#2)

Breaking Away (#3)

Breaking Free (#4)

Breaking Hearts (#5)

Breaking Ties (#6)

Breaking Point (#7)

Visit ellejames.com for titles and release dates

For hot cowboys, visit her alter ego Myla Jackson at mylajackson.com

and join Elle James's Newsletter at https://ellejames.com/contact/

CHAPTER 1

"WHAT ARE you doing behind the bar?" Jim "Sarge" Walker emerged from the kitchen of the Salty Dog Saloon, carrying a tray loaded with hamburgers and fries. Sweat pebbled his bald brow as he frowned in her direction.

Sophia Phillips grinned. "Looked like you could use a little help. Where's Mags?"

Sarge grimaced. "She's running late. Today is her day to get her nails done. You know how that goes."

Sophia shook her head. Mags's number one priority was to look good. At fifty-one years old, she wasn't growing old without a fight.

Sarge put up with her being late because she was good at what she did. Mags was an excellent waitress, and she kept things running smoothly in the saloon.

"You didn't answer my question," Sarge said as he strode by with the tray of food.

"I thought I'd help myself to a drink while waiting for my friends."

"While you're there, you can help me with a couple mugs of beers from the tap for the two men at table six."

Sophia chuckled. "Gotcha." She positioned a mug beneath the tap and pulled the handle forward. After that mug filled, she set another beneath the tap and filled it as well. When both mugs were full, she carried them to table six.

"Hey, Red, when are you gonna marry me?" asked one of the two men.

Sophia's lips twisted. "What would your wife have to say, Joe?"

Joe grinned. "What she doesn't know won't hurt her."

"Yeah." Sophia pressed her lips together. "Don't be a dumbass. Becky's the best thing that ever happened to you."

"Yeah, but she isn't a redhead like you," Joe said.

"Be nice to her," Sophia said. "She might take off with a better man and leave you in her dust."

"I'm not married," the other man said. "When are you gonna marry me?"

"Never in a million years, Randy."

"You cut me to the core," Randy said, clutching his heart.

She collected their empties and loaded her tray. "I'm sure the bleeding will stop soon." Sophia turned as a woman with sandy-blond hair and blue eyes entered the saloon, wearing blue medical scrubs.

Sophia smiled. "Hey, Beth."

Beth pulled a rubber band out of her hair, smiled and waved at her across the room. "Hey, Sophia. I thought you weren't working tonight."

"I'm not," Sophia said. "I'm just filling the gap until Mags gets here."

"Good, because we're celebrating." Beth stretched her arms over her head and arched her back. "I could use a Painkiller, if you want to mix one up for me."

"I heard the guys were back from deployment." A thrill of excitement rippled through Sophia's body.

"When did they get in?" Beth asked.

"Last night. I heard Blade's truck door slam after I went to bed."

"And did you run out to see him?" Beth asked with a teasing grin.

Sophia shook her head. "I was already in bed, or I might have. I figured we'd see them tonight. I know Nora and Layla are probably beside themselves."

"I saw Nora's car pull into the parking lot as I walked in. Layla's riding with her," Beth said. "They should be coming through the door about now."

Sophia glanced past Beth. "They're here."

Beth grinned. "Now, all we need is the guys. I'm betting they're ready for a little R & R."

"Speaking of which," Sophia said, "are we still on for the trip to Cancún?"

"About that…" Beth started and paused as she glanced toward the two women entering the bar.

Nora and Layla stepped through the door and turned toward another woman entering behind them.

"I didn't know Kylie was going to make it," Sophia said.

"Me either. She must be back from her latest news assignment."

Nora Michaels, wearing her nurse's scrubs, hugged Kylie.

Layla took her turn hugging the woman next. The three women made their way across the room to the bar, where Beth and Sophia stood.

Nora smiled. "We're all here. Where are the guys?"

"I got a text a few minutes ago." Kylie held up her cellphone. "Mac said they got stuck in a debriefing with their commander. He's convinced they'll all get in trouble since they're on leave. He wants to make sure they don't do anything stupid."

"What are the chances of that?" Nora grinned.

Kylie nodded. "I know. They're all a bunch of adrenaline junkies. If they don't stay busy, they'll get bored pretty quickly."

"And boredom leads to…" Sophia waited for all the women to chime in.

"Trouble!" Sophia, Layla, Kylie, Nora and Beth said at once.

"Someone call my name?" a deep voice called out from the saloon entrance.

Sophia's heart fluttered as she glanced across the barroom at the man who'd captured her heart from the moment he'd first walked into the Salty Dog Saloon over a year ago. The man who was now her next-door neighbor, and the man who didn't know she existed, other than as a waitress, bartender and a friend.

The friend zone sucked.

She sighed and willed her pulse to slow to a normal rate.

Michael Calhoun, or Blade, had the blackest hair and the bluest eyes of any man Sophia had ever seen. He could have any woman he wanted, and usually did...have any woman who caught his eye.

Unfortunately, that didn't include Sophia. Still, her heart fluttered, and her body flushed all over.

Blade opened his arms. "Can a guy get a welcome home hug around here?" His gaze landed on Sophia as he crossed the bar to where she stood with the other women.

"If you're not going to hug the man, I sure as hell am." Beth stepped into Blade's arms. "Welcome home, soldier," she said with a smile and leaned up on her toes to press a kiss to Blade's lips.

Heat rushed into Sophia's cheeks, and her fingers curled into her palms to keep from scratching Beth's eyes out. Some friend she was.

Then again, Blade hadn't singled out any one woman with his comment.

He hugged Beth and set her to the side. Then Blade looked at the other ladies standing close by. "What? Is Beth the only one who's happy to see me?"

"Of course not," Nora Michaels said. She crossed to Blade, gave him a short hug, and then looked over his shoulder and exclaimed, "Rucker, you're here!" She ran into her fiancé's arms.

"I'm glad to see you." Layla gave Blade a quick hug and hurried past him to throw herself into Craig Bullington's arms.

"Good to see you, Blade." Kylie Adams waved as she rushed past him to Sean "Mac" McDaniel, leaving Sophia standing by herself.

With the rest of his team filing in behind him, Blade moved a few steps forward, stopping in front of Sophia. "Hey."

Heat rose up Sophia's neck, filling her cheeks. "Hey, yourself."

Blade took a step toward her. "I didn't see you at the airport last night."

Sophia forced a shrug. "I had to work."

"Surely your boss would've let you off to welcome me home after being deployed for so many months."

"I'm sure he would have," she said, "had you been a fiancé or a spouse. I didn't even think to ask."

Blade cocked an eyebrow. "Good friends don't count?"

"Sure, they do." She couldn't hold back any longer. She walked up to him, put her arms around his neck and hugged him. God, she'd missed him. His arms settled around her waist. She leaned into him for just a moment, inhaling the sexy outdoorsy scent of him. As quickly as she hugged him, she stepped back. She couldn't let herself get used to holding him. "Good to see you, Blade."

"Wow," he said, "that was almost a hug."

She shot him a tight smile. "Can I get you a beer?"

He nodded.

She didn't ask him what kind. Sophia knew what he liked. She slipped behind the counter and drew a draft beer in a mug for him. The rest of the guys and the women stepped up to the bar, and she filled their orders as well.

"You missed the big engagement last night at the airport," Nora said.

Sophia's head popped up. "Really? Which one of you?"

"Bull asked me." Layla raised her hand, displaying a diamond on her ring finger. "I said yes."

"It was all very beautiful," Nora said. "You should've been there."

"I had to work," Sophia insisted.

"No, you didn't," Sarge said. "Mags was here last night. She would've covered for you."

Trust Sarge to walk by and open his mouth at just

the wrong moment. "Why don't y'all get a table? I'll bring the drinks over," Sophia said.

"But you're not working tonight," Beth said.

"No, I'm just filling in for Mags until she gets here." She waved a hand. "Go on. Find a table."

Beth was the last one to turn. "Why didn't you come last night?"

Sophia filled another mug with beer. "I didn't feel like I'd fit in."

"What are you talking about? We're all a part of this little group."

"Yeah, but most of the women already have their guys, and I don't."

"Neither do I," Beth said.

"Yeah, but you and Nora are close friends."

"We're not?" Beth asked.

Sophia smiled. "We're getting there. After all, I did invite you to go to Cancún with me."

Beth grinned. "Yes, you did. I'd like to think you wouldn't have invited just anybody."

Sophia glanced across the barroom to where Blade was pulling a seat out at one of the tables. "No, I wouldn't ask just anybody."

Beth turned to see where Sophia was looking. "Still friend-zoned?"

Sophia sighed. "Yes."

"When's that man going to wake up and see what he's got right in front of him?"

"Never. I'm not his type."

Beth turned toward her. “And what type is that?”

“The gorgeous, sophisticated type.”

Beth snorted. “Ha! Sweetheart, you’re gorgeous.”

Sophia grimaced and touched a hand to her strawberry-blond hair. “Not even close,” Sophia said. “This red hair. These freckles. All men ever see me as is the kid sister or the girl next door. I’m literally the girl next door for Blade.”

“You would think that would make him a little more aware of you as a woman not just the girl next door, by living next door to him.”

“Yeah, you’d think,” Sophia said. “It’s what I get for letting him know about the house that was for sale next to me.”

“Living so close, should have given you more time to get to know each other.”

“When he’s not deployed, we do spend time together out in our backyards. However, he’s never so much as kissed me. Face it, I’m stuck.”

“What do you mean stuck?” Beth said.

“He’ll never look at me as anything other than the girl next door or the friend who’s always there. The worst part about it is, when he does bring a woman home, I just eat my heart out. Now that he lives next to me, I’m going to have to find another house and move away.”

“Surely it’s not that bad.”

“How would you like it if the man you cared

about brought a woman home, married her, and had children with her right next door to you?"

Beth grimaced. "Well, when you put it that way… Yeah, I guess it is pretty bad. Just think, maybe you'll meet somebody in Cancún and forget all about Blade."

"I'm really not interested in meeting anybody. I just need some time away to decide what I'm going to do with the rest of my life. Maybe it's time I quit the bar and put my degree to use."

"Oh, sweetie. Accounting would be so boring."

"Yeah, but it would probably pay better than the tips I get here."

"I thought you got some pretty good tips."

Sophia grinned. "I do. And I never really wanted to become an accountant. My parents talked me into that degree. No, I'm not going on a manhunt in Cancún. I'm just going to relax and enjoy the sun, the sand and the water." She filled the last mug, set it on a tray and lifted it into her arms. "Let's go join the others."

Beth's eyes narrowed as Sophia passed her. "Girl, we gotta get that man to really notice you."

"That'll never happen. Come on, let's go enjoy some time with everyone." Sophia carried the tray of drinks across to the couple of tables they'd pulled together, and they all sat around. They passed out their drinks.

When everybody had one in hand, Nora raised

hers. "To the guys. We're so very glad you came back, all in one piece."

Sophia lifted her glass. "Here, here."

Rucker lifted his mug. "And to the ladies who were here to greet us when we got home. Thank you for keeping the home fires burning."

The men all lifted their mugs. "Here, here." They all took a drink and settled in.

"So, what have you guys been up to since we've been gone?" Dawg asked.

Beth grinned. "Sophia won a trip to Cancún."

All eyes turned to Sophia.

Blade said, "Really?"

She nodded. "Yeah, I got an all-expense paid trip by signing up at the local home and garden show."

"She leaves in two days," Beth said.

"*We* leave in two days," Sophia corrected.

"Oh, so Beth's going with you?" Blade asked.

Sophia nodded. "Yup."

"Sounds like fun," Blade said.

Beth frowned. "Well, you know, Sophia, I meant to tell you. I got a call just before I got here."

Sophia frowned. "From whom?"

"From my Aunt Petunia. She's in the hospital and, uh, I'm afraid I'm going to have to back out of the trip."

Sophia frowned. "You can't back out on me now. We leave in two days."

"Can't you reschedule?" Beth asked.

"No, the dates are set in stone. I leave in two days, or I forfeit the trip."

Beth gave her a forlorn look. "Well, maybe you can find somebody to take my place."

"At the last minute?" Sophia asked, her voice rising.

Beth glanced around the table. "Yeah, I'm sure there's one of us, or maybe one of you guys. I mean you're all on leave, right? Surely somebody can take the time off to go with Sophia to Cancún."

Sophia shook her head. "I don't even know if they'll let me exchange a name at this late date. And it would have to be somebody with a passport. You've got your passport."

"And so do all the guys," Beth pointed out. "What about you, Dawg? Don't you want an all-expense paid trip to Cancún with Sophia?"

Dawg grinned. "Oh, hell yeah."

Blade smacked his mug on the table. "Oh, hell no, you don't. If anyone's going with Sophia, it's going to be me, rather than any of you other horndogs."

Dawg said, "Why should she go with you? You're the biggest womanizer of all of us."

"Exactly, she should go with me because I'm not interested."

Sophia wanted to reach across the table and smack him.

"She's my neighbor—and my friend. I've never even thought about dating her. I'd be the safest bet."

"Well, I hadn't thought about dating her," Dawg said, "until now." He waggled his brows at Sophia.

Sophia grinned, although her heart pounded at the thought of Blade offering to take Beth's place on the trip. "Seriously," she said, "I don't know if we can make a replacement at this late a date. It's only two days from now. I'll just have to go by myself."

"The hell you are," Blade said. "As your friend, I can't allow that. Mexico isn't always a safe place. You need a buddy to go along with you. Somebody who's got your back."

"Yeah, but if you go with me, you'll be off flirting with somebody else."

"I'll flirt, but I'll keep an eye on you."

Sophia shook her head. "No, I'd be better off going by myself."

Blade looked to Beth. "Beth, talk some sense into your friend."

Beth shook her head. "She's your friend, too. You convince her. I have to take care of my aunt."

Sophia looked at her friend narrow-eyed. "Aunt Petunia, huh?"

Beth raised her chin. "Yup. She never liked her name. We all love her anyway."

"Look, Sophia," Blade said, "I promise I'll keep an eye on you, and you can keep an eye on me. That's what friends do for each other." He held up his hand. "I swear, I won't take any other woman to bed before I see you tucked into yours."

Sophia's lips twisted. "Thanks," she said and under her breath muttered, "for nothing."

"So, it's decided?" Beth asked.

"What? What's decided?" Sophia asked.

"That Blade's going to go with you to Cancún."

Blade nodded.

Sophia shook her head. "I don't know. I don't think it's a good idea."

"Me either," said Rucker.

Blade glared at the man and kicked him beneath the table.

"Ouch!" Rucker frowned. "Why'd you kick me?"

Blade glared back at him. "Why'd you say it was a bad idea?"

"We all like Sophia," Rucker said. "We don't want to see her hurt by you."

Blade held up his hands. "She's my friend. She's also my next-door neighbor. I'm not going to screw up our friendship when she lives right next door to me. Besides, Sophia's the marrying kind."

"What do you mean by that?" Sophia asked.

"You're the kind of woman a man wants to marry."

Her lips twisted. "Whatever."

"And I'm not ever getting married."

"Famous last words," Mac said as he grinned across the table at Layla. He reached for his fiancée's hand and twirled the ring around her finger. "Apparently, you haven't met the right woman yet."

"That's not the case. I just don't plan on ever getting married. As a Delta, it just doesn't make sense. And why would I screw up a perfectly good friendship marrying her or taking her to bed?"

Mac frowned. "How do we know you won't try to get into Sophia's pants while you're in Cancún?"

Sophia gasped. "Wow, did you really ask that?"

Beth backhanded Mac.

"Yeah, we like Sophia," Lance said. "We like the Salty Dog Saloon. We don't wanna see her leave."

"Look," Blade said, "I care about Sophia too, and I don't want to see her hurt while she's down in Mexico. I could keep a close eye on her, without putting my hands on her. Like I said, she's the girl next door. I don't want to screw that up."

Sophia's lips pressed into a thin line, and her eyes narrowed. "What if I don't want you to go with me? What if I'd rather have Dawg take me?"

Dawg grinned. "I'm ready and willing." He leaned over and planted a kiss on her cheek. "Just think of the good times we'd have."

Blade glared at Dawg. "You can't trust that man. If you want to have a good time in Cancún and not worry about somebody pawing all over you, take me. I could use a vacation, and you could use some protection. You choose."

The men at the table chanted, "Dawg! Dawg! Dawg! Dawg!"

And the women said, "Blade! Blade! Blade! Blade!"

Sophia shook her head. "I'm not making a decision. Not with all this noise. Anybody need another drink? I'm going to get a refill."

"You haven't drunk what you have."

She tipped her mug up, swallowed the contents and smacked it down on the table. "Like I said, I'm going for a refill. Anybody else?"

"While you're up, I'll take another."

"Me, too."

"And me."

She gathered the empties on a tray and carried them back to the bar.

Beth followed. "You're not seriously considering Dawg, are you?"

Sophia glared at Beth. "I can't believe you just backed out on this trip."

Beth grinned. "You have the perfect opportunity to get some alone time with Blade. With none of the other guys around. You won't be next door. You'll be out on your own."

"You heard him. He's not interested in me. You know what kind of torture that will be?"

"It might help get him out of your system. Who knows? Maybe you'll figure out he really does care about you as more than just a friend."

"It's bad enough when he brings women to his house. I don't think I could stand it if I'm in Cancún with him as he's flirting with another woman."

Beth quirked her lip. "Turn it around on him. You flirt with somebody else."

Sophia shook her head. "I'm not interested in anybody else."

Her friend crossed her arms over her chest. "Well, maybe it's about time you should be."

Sophia stared across the barroom at Blade. Maybe that was it. Maybe if she made him jealous, he might actually think of her as something other than the girl next door. The friend. If that didn't work, then… well…she knew she had to get over him.

Sophia sighed. "Okay. But promise me you'll never pull some shit like this again."

Beth grinned. "You'll be thanking me someday."

"Yeah," Sophia said, "that day isn't today." She filled their drink order as Mags walked through the front door.

"Let me get that," the older woman said.

Sophia needed something to keep her hands busy. "No, I've got this. I'm sure that Sarge has other orders for you to fill." She carried the tray back to the table and stared across at Blade. "Okay, if we can get the names changed, Blade's going with me."

Blade grinned. "Smart choice."

"Yeah, damn," Dawg said. "I had my tastebuds set for some good Mexican food, Mai Tais and Painkillers."

"Guess I better buy some swim shorts, dust off my

passport and make some phone calls." Blade clapped his hands. "I'm going to Mexico."

Sophia's heart beat fast. She stared across at the man. She was probably setting herself up for a big fall, but it was about time that she either got him to notice her or got over him.

BLADE SAT across the table from Sophia, sipping his beer, his mind on a million things at once. He was used to deploying at the drop of a hat, but he'd never gone on vacation this spontaneously. It didn't matter. The thought of Sophia going by herself was not acceptable. To tell the truth, he would've preferred to stay home and sip beer in his backyard with her, rather than go all the way to Cancún, Mexico.

But if she was going, and alone, he felt responsible, as her friend, to be with her and provide the protection she'd need. Tourists never knew what would happen in Mexico. With her cute redhaired looks, she would be a prime target for sex traffickers. He wished he could bring his gun with him. Blade was glad Beth had backed out of the trip. The thought of the two women by themselves in Mexico would have made him crazy. He might have bought his own ticket and flown down there just to make sure they were okay.

The ladies all got up and went to the bathroom together, giving the men time to talk.

Dawg wadded up a napkin and threw it at Blade. "I almost had a free trip to Cancún. Why'd you have to go and ruin it for me?"

"Sophia deserves somebody better than you," Blade said.

He snorted. "And that ain't you."

"He's right," Rucker said. "Seriously, I hope you're not planning on seducing her."

Blade's mouth pressed into a thin line. "I'm not going to seduce Sophia. I'm going to take care of her and make sure that nobody seduces her or takes advantage of her. She's like a kid sister to me." At that moment, the women were headed back across the room, and Blade's gaze landed on Sophia.

Apparently, Dawg's did too. "She's not *my* kid sister and she's got a body that won't quit. Topped with that red hair…wow."

"Keep it in your pants, Dawg," Blade warned. "She's a nice girl. Leave her alone."

"You're not interested in her," Dawg said, "but maybe I am."

Blade narrowed his eyes. "Back off. She chose me as her protector, not as a boyfriend. If she was thinking of you as a boyfriend, she would've chosen you."

"All right," Rucker said. "We're holding you accountable, Blade. Treat her right or answer to us."

"I will." Blade held up one hand. "I promise."

"In the meantime," John Sanders, otherwise

known as Tank, said, "what are we going to do on our leave time?"

"Since I'm not going to Cancún, I'm going to sleep for twenty-four hours," Dawg said. "After that, I might drive down to South Padre and get some sun and sand."

"I'm spending my leave with my girl." Bull nodded toward the dark-haired beauty heading his way.

Mac waved a hand at Kylie. "Same here."

Dash grinned. "I'm meeting Sunny Daye in Dallas. I have a hotel booked and room service lined up."

Blade leaned back in his chair with a grin. "I'm going to Cancún."

"Watch out," Dawg said. "We might all decide to join you."

Blade patted his chest confidently. "It would be all right with me. Then I could prove to you that I'm not going to do anything but protect Sophia."

CHAPTER 2

"MA'AM, can I get you anything to drink?" The flight attendant stopped beside Sophia's seat.

Though the plane was small, she was flying first class to Houston, and then from Houston she'd fly to Cancún. Again, first class. Winning a trip had its perks.

"No, thank you." Sophia stared out the window, her pulse pounding. Where was he? The boarding call had been completed, and Blade had yet to enter the plane. Sophia had waited as long as she could, but then she'd had to board. All the other seats were filled on the small aircraft in Temple, Texas, except the one beside her.

The flight attendant stepped outside the airplane and came back in smiling and talking to someone. When Sophia saw the someone, she sighed.

Thank God.

Blade strolled onto the plane, a smile spreading across his face as he spied her. He took his seat on the opposite side of the aisle from Sophia.

They were on a regional plane that would take them from Temple to Houston, and it only had fourteen seats. With all fourteen seats filled, the door was closed.

"I knew we should've ridden together," Sophia grumbled.

Blade gave her a crooked smile. "Sorry about that. I had to sign out of my unit. As I was leaving, my commander decided he needed to give me a lecture on how to behave in Mexico."

Sophia frowned. "Does he do that for *all* the guys in the unit?"

Blade's mouth turned up on one corner. "No, he thought I was a special case and needed an extra lecture."

"From experience?" Sophia asked.

Blade shrugged. "Most likely."

Sophia sat back in her seat and let the tension drain out of her. "Well, at least you made it. I was beginning to think I was going to make this trip on my own."

"I hurried. As soon as my commander cut me loose, I put the lead on the accelerator to get to the airport on time. They almost didn't let me onto the airplane, but I sweet-talked the gate attendant."

Sophia cocked an eyebrow. "Female?"

Blade grinned. "Yup."

"Figures," Sophia muttered. Who could resist the man? That dark hair, ice-blue eyes and those muscles.

Ugh.

Sophia could relate.

The flight to Houston didn't take long, and soon they were hustling across the airport to get to their next plane. Once they were settled in first class, Sophia could finally relax. They were seated in the center section of business class on the 747. Sophia had chosen the aisle seat. A pretty, sultry, dark-haired woman sat on the other side of Blade, making Sophia wish she had chosen the seat where Blade was sitting.

Blade immediately engaged in conversation with the woman, even before the plane took off. At least a handsome young man with dark hair and deep brown eyes sat in the seat across the aisle from Sophia.

The woman beside Blade laughed, making Sophia's teeth grind. What did she have to do to get Blade to notice her like he noticed the pretty, dark-haired woman? She couldn't change her hair. She was stuck with strawberry-blond. She couldn't change her complexion without a ton of makeup. That was something she wasn't willing to do. Maybe Beth was right, and all she needed to do was show him that someone else could appreciate her and find her attractive. Maybe that would make him jealous enough to look at her as other than *just a friend.* Pasting a smile on her face, she looked across the aisle at the good-looking guy.

"Are you going on vacation?" she asked.

The dark-haired man shook his head and smiled back at her. "No, I'm headed home. I live in the Cancún area," he said with a Hispanic accent that would melt most women's knees.

If Sophia wasn't so hung up on Blade, she might have found this guy incredibly attractive. Maybe she should make more of an effort to try. That might not be a bad thing. Either the jealousy thing would work, or Sophia would have to move on. Why not move on with a sexy Mexican with a voice that would melt butter?

For the next few hours, she spent her time talking with the young man whose name ended up being Andrés Manuel Calderón, a native Mexican who'd been on a business trip in the US.

A few times she glanced toward Blade. She noticed him frowning in her direction, but he quickly turned and smiled at the woman beside him and kept up the conversation. Meanwhile, Andrés entertained her with what she might find to do in Cancún.

"You could do all the things tourists do like a catamaran trip to Isla Mujeres, which can be fun. Or a trip out to the Mayan ruins of Chichen Itza to climb

El Castillo, also known as the Temple of Kukulcán. I recommend both excursions."

"But tonight, there's a celebration in downtown Cancún for *Cinco de Mayo.* You should come. There will be music and dancing."

"I'd like that," Sophia said.

"I could pick you up from your hotel," he said, "and you could come with me. I know all the places to go."

Sophia grimaced. "That would be nice, but I think it would be best if I meet you downtown. My friend, Blade, and I could join you there." She tipped her head toward Blade.

"What was that?" Blade asked. "I heard my name. I hope it wasn't spoken in vain."

Sophia turned to Blade and smiled. "Blade, this is Andrés Calderón. Andrés, this is Blade. We were just talking about meeting up in downtown Cancún for the annual *Cinco de Mayo* celebration."

"Don't you think we should discuss this before you make plans?" Blade asked with a frown.

"We're discussing it now," she said. "I think it's a good idea. I'd like to meet with Andrés downtown. He's promised me music and dancing."

Blade's frown deepened.

"If you don't want to come," Sophia said, "Andrés said that he would pick me up at the hotel. Either way, I'd like to go to the celebration."

"I'll bring her," Blade said, leveling a stare at Andrés.

"Then it's settled," Andrés said. "I'll meet you downtown at eight o'clock in front of the cathedral."

"Won't it be packed?" Sophia asked.

Andrés shrugged. "It will, but I'll be able to pick you out. I can't miss that red hair amongst the crowd. It's beautiful."

Sophia's cheeks heated.

"Don't you think?" Andrés asked Blade.

Blade stared across at Sophia, his eyes narrowing. "Of course." He stared at her for a long moment.

Sophia felt like he was seeing her for the first time. When he'd said 'of course', she'd wanted to kick him. The man wasn't impressed with the uniqueness of her hair. She might not succeed at getting him jealous. In that case, she would need to learn to enjoy others' company, and she could start with Andrés.

When they landed, Andrés was first out of his seat. He helped Sophia with her carryon, pulling it out from the overhead bin. He smiled and, lifting her hand, pressed his lips to her knuckles. "Until tonight."

She had hoped that her heart would flutter like it did whenever she saw Blade, but it didn't. Perhaps with time it would. It didn't matter. She was determined to have a good time in Cancún with or without Blade.

As soon as they cleared the sky bridge, the passengers were split up by Mexican citizens and all others. Sophia and Blade said their goodbyes to their conversation partners and navigated the customs lines. When they emerged from the airport, a man dressed in a black suit, holding a sign with Sophia's name on it, stood waiting next to a black limousine.

"Now, that's what I call riding in style." Blade grinned and tossed their luggage into the trunk.

The chauffeur opened the door for Sophia, and she slid into the backseat. Blade climbed in next to her. It was the first time since they'd gotten on the plane in Houston that they were alone, except for the chauffeur.

"About tonight," Blade started.

Sophia pinned a smile on her face. "What about it? I am so excited, I can't wait. I've never been to an authentic *Cinco de Mayo* celebration."

He frowned. "Yeah, about that. I'm not so sure it's a good idea."

"Why not?" Sophia asked, her heartbeat picking up. Was he maybe just a little bit jealous?

"All of the resorts are fairly safe. Anywhere outside of the resorts, not so much. They have drug cartels operating throughout Mexico. For all you know, Andrés Calderón could be a member."

Sophia snorted. "Are you sure you're not jealous because I talked with him all the way from Houston?"

"Of course not," Blade said.

Sophia's heart plummeted. "Is it because you don't have a date for the *Cinco de Mayo* celebration? Why didn't you ask the young lady who was sitting next to you on the plane?"

Blade snorted. "I would have, but I imagine her husband would've been less than agreeable."

Sophia frowned. "What about the flight attendant? I'm sure they have a layover tonight."

He shook his head. "She's spending time with her family in Cancún."

"Well, maybe you'll meet somebody at the celebration tonight, because," Sophia lifted her chin, "with or without you, I'm going."

"I'm going with you. Remember, I'm your bodyguard, so don't try to ditch me."

"I won't try to ditch you as long as you understand that you're not my chaperone. However, the very handsome and gentlemanly Andrés Calderón and I plan on drinking margaritas and dancing until past midnight. Are you up for that?"

"I can handle it." Blade shrugged. "It can't be worse than facing the Taliban in a ten-to-one firefight."

Sophia laughed. "Surely, it won't be as bad as that."

"Hopefully not. However, drug cartels have been known to fire into crowds. I suggest we keep our exit routes in mind."

The driver pulled up to the resort reception area and unloaded their luggage from the trunk. He whisked them up to the check-in line and left their luggage with the bellman.

A clerk in a white guayabera shirt, with a nametag announcing him as Guillermo, smiled broadly. "*Buenos días, Señorita Phillips*. We are so happy to welcome you to Playa del Luna."

"*Gracias*." She returned his smile. "I believe we have a suite with two queen-size beds?"

The man checked his computer terminal and frowned. He clicked a few keys, his eyes narrowed and then his frown turned upside down into an expansive smile. "I'm pleased to say you've been upgraded to a bungalow in one of our premiere locations located near the beach."

"That's lovely," Sophia said. "With two queen-size beds?"

"No, Senorita Phillips. I am most pleased to say it has a king-size bed with a view of the water, a large living area with sofas and a dining table and your own private veranda."

Though the bungalow sounded amazing, Sophia's gut clenched. "Is one of the sofas a fold-out bed?"

The man frowned and looked down at his computer terminal again. "I'm afraid not." He grinned again. "But I'm sure that you and your guest will be comfortable in the king-size bed."

"But—" Sophia started.

Blade cupped her elbow and smiled across at the clerk. "Thank you very much. We'll need two sets of keys and someone to bring our luggage to the bungalow."

The clerk switched his attention to Blade and handed over the keys with a smile. "Enjoy your visit. If there's anything you need, please don't hesitate to ask."

As Blade guided her away from the reception desk, Sophia muttered, "I need a room with two queen-size beds. I didn't plan on having to share the bed with you."

"I'm sure the couch will be just fine. It'll be nice to have a room with a view of the water. Let's just get there and assess."

A bellman wheeled a cart with their luggage along a path leading out of the main hotel then along a walkway with bungalows on each side. When he reached the end, he paused in front of the last one.

Sophia's breath caught as she stared out at the ocean.

The bellman grinned. "It is *muy bueno, si?*"

"Yes," Sophia said. "It is *muy bueno.*"

The bellman unlocked the door and set their luggage inside.

Blade tipped the man, and he left with the cart. Blade urged Sophia to enter. "This is much nicer than being in the main hotel."

Sophia nodded. Every window had a view. "You could put up with a lot for that view, but I get the bed." She glanced around the bungalow, noticing that there were several chairs—and one small sofa. She pulled the cushions off the sofa. "Damn. The clerk was right. There's no fold-out bed in here."

Blade lifted a shoulder. "Don't worry. I'll make do."

Sophia shook her head. There was no way. The man would hang four feet off the couch. "You can't sleep on that. I'll take the couch, and you can have the king-size bed."

"I'll be fine," Blade said. "If anything, I can sleep on the floor. I've slept on worse."

She frowned. "Yeah, but you're here on vacation. Not in a foxhole."

Blade headed toward the veranda. "I could sleep out on the deck on one of the lounge chairs. They'll be better than an Army cot."

"We'll see," Sophia said. "In the meantime, I plan on hitting the waves." She snagged her suitcase and rolled it into the single bathroom. "I'll only be a minute."

Sophia slipped out of her clothes, doused herself thoroughly with sunscreen, and stepped into the royal blue bikini Beth had chosen for her to wear. She wished she'd brought the one-piece. The bikini was far too revealing.

She stared at herself in the mirror and frowned. Her pale skin would blind anybody in the sunshine. Why couldn't she have the dark olive-toned skin of the woman who'd sat next to Blade the entire trip from Houston to Cancún?

Well, the sunscreen would have to do its job, but she'd need some help putting it on her back. The thought of Blade smoothing his hands over her skin made her shiver in anticipation. Of course, he still thought of her as only a friend, but she could live in her own fantasy as he smoothed the cream across her skin.

She plunked a broad-brimmed hat on her head, pulled a cover-up over her shoulders and fished a beach towel out of the closet. With her sunscreen and towel in hand, she emerged from the bathroom.

Blade stood in the middle of the room wearing a pair of swim trunks and nothing else but flip flops on his feet. He grinned. "Ready to go?"

Sophia nodded, wishing that she'd come just a little earlier out of the bathroom to catch him changing from his street clothes to his swim trunks. Her breath lodged in her throat. Damn he was sexy. With his deeply tanned, broad shoulders, he could have modeled for one of those men's athletic magazines. He turned his smile toward her.

Her knees melted. Who was she kidding? This man could never be interested in the redhaired, pale-skinned, freckle-faced girl next door as anything other than a friend. Resigned to her position as Blade's friend, she nodded. "Let's go."

All they had to do was walk straight out of the bungalow and onto the beach. After anchoring their beach towels with their flip flops, the moment of reckoning came. Sophia really wished that she had that one-piece swimsuit now. Maybe even a full wetsuit to cover her pale skin. She took a deep breath, sighed and dropped her coverup and her hat on the beach towel.

Blade smiled and shook his head. "Sweetheart, you can't stay out here very long. That sun will cook your skin."

She slapped the tube of sunscreen into his hands. "Then do me the honors and get my back. I got everywhere else I could reach."

"My pleasure," he said, and he squirted the thick lotion into his palms and rubbed them together. "Turn around."

She obeyed, her heart skipping several beats before her pulse pounded through her veins.

His hands descended on her shoulders, their warmth seeping into her skin, shooting heat all the way to her core. As he smoothed his hands over her skin, she closed her eyes and fantasized that he was her lover, that he liked pale skin and freckle-faced girls with red hair. His hands moved from her shoulders down the center of her back. Moving in a circular motion, he dipped further south to the elastic band of her string bikini. He lingered there.

Desire rippled through Sophia.

He leaned close to her ear. "Did you get the backs of your thighs?"

She sucked in a breath and shook her head. "No."

His hands skimmed over her buttocks, and he smoothed cream over the backs of her thighs up to her butt cheeks that weren't covered by the bikini. *Holy hell,* she thought. *I'm going to climax, and we're not even making love.* Her breath caught and held, body tingling.

Then his hands left her body. He capped the tube and tossed it onto the beach towel. "Last one in is a rotten egg," he said, and ran toward the water.

Sophia spent a minute standing there watching as he dove into the waves. She let her pulse return to normal and the heat abate just a little before she followed him into the water.

Taking it more slowly, she waded in up to her waist.

Blade went under and, for a moment, she couldn't see him. Sophia spun in a circle. She couldn't find him, and she worried when he didn't come up. Something grabbed her ankles and yanked her feet out from under her. She dipped below the surface and came up sputtering in front of a laughing Blade.

Game on!

For the next fifteen minutes, they played in the water dunking each other. Blade picked her up and threw her into the surf several times as if she weighed nothing. They laughed and teased each other like a couple of teenagers.

Sophia found herself relaxing in his company. So, they might not be lovers, but he did make a good friend and he was fun to be with. She could be satisfied with that at least for the week they'd be in Cancún. And who knew? Maybe friends could turn to lovers? It was one of her favorite tropes in the books she read. Sophia could only hope.

CHAPTER 3

WHEN THEY'D HAD enough saltwater, Blade secured a couple of lounge chairs and a beach umbrella. He was concerned that Sophia would burn in the hot Cancún sun, and he'd hate to see her beautiful pale skin turn red and blotchy, knowing how painful it would be.

Once he had her seated in the shade, he went off to find a couple of drinks. All the while he was away from her, he kept her in his sight. Blade found a waiter, gave his order and returned to where Sophia lay with her eyes closed on the lounge chair, her beautiful body drying in the gentle breeze.

She wasn't his usual type, which was a good thing. She was his friend and his next-door neighbor. He shouldn't be thinking about her as anything else.

But seeing her lying there in her royal blue bikini that left very little to the imagination, his pulse quickened, and his groin tightened. He'd never considered her as anything other than a friend.

His reputation with the women was one he'd earned. Mr. "Love 'em and Leave 'em" Blade. As long as he was a Delta he didn't want to commit. He would only end up breaking her heart or his. The thought of falling in love, and then the woman falling out of love with him, kept him from wanting a permanent relationship, especially as much as the Deltas deployed. He hated to think of leaving a woman behind to fend for herself. He wouldn't be there to protect her from harm. He wouldn't be there to help her when she was sick. And if she had children, he wouldn't be there to help her change diapers and go to ballgames or dance lessons with them.

Too many of his friends within the Delta Force had learned the hard way that most women wouldn't tolerate a man who was gone all the time. People got lonely. Sophia deserved a man who would be there for her. A man who would love and protect her.

She put up with a lot of shit with her job as a bartender and waitress, but she always had a smile on her face. When she laughed, her eyes sparkled. She was an amazing woman and merited being happy.

Blade wasn't the man who could give her that happiness.

Still, he couldn't help relaxing in her company and enjoying the time they had together. He could do this. He could be her friend. As long as he didn't have to smear lotion on her back too often. Whew. That, in itself, had been a challenge. He'd run into the water just to tamp down the hard-on he'd gotten.

He wasn't hers, and he had no claim on Sophia, but he wasn't excited about her meeting another man in downtown Cancún. He told himself he wasn't excited about it because he was afraid of crime outside the resort. Even more afraid that members of a drug cartel might show up and gun down innocents.

More than that, he didn't trust this Andrés Calderón. As soon as he got back to the hotel, he'd give his buddies a call and have them do some research, and maybe see if there was anything on Caldron that would put up any red flags. If he had a history of drugs and violence, then maybe Blade could convince Sophia not to go downtown for the *Cinco de Mayo* celebration.

When the waiter came with their drinks, Blade handed one to Sophia.

She pushed to a sitting position and smiled as she reached out for the drink. "What did you get me?"

"I thought we'd start the vacation with Painkillers."

"Mmm, it looks lovely." She sipped her drink. "And it tastes great. Thank you."

"What do you want to do while we're here? I mean, besides hanging out on the beach, at the pool and soaking up the sun?"

"Andrés was telling me about some of the excursions available from here. I thought maybe we could do a catamaran trip out to Isla Mujeres. I've never snorkeled anywhere but off the beaches at South Padre."

Blade ginned. "You're going to love it. The water is so much clearer, and there's so much to see, sea life and coral."

"Good. We'll do that. We need to talk to the concierge and get that on our schedule."

"I'd like to make a trip out to Chichen Itza," Blade said. "I've been there before, but I'd like to explore it again. I think you would love it."

"That's right," Sophia grinned. "That's another place Andrés mentioned. From the pictures it looks amazing. I'm game for that as well."

The mention of Andrés made Blade tense. He'd wait for some feedback from his friends before he tried to talk Sophia out of meeting the man in downtown Cancún. He needed ammunition to talk her out of the rendezvous. In the meantime, he would enjoy the sun, the smell of the salt in the air and lying next to a beautiful woman—along with a constant reminder that she was strictly a friend.

"Are you hungry?" Sophia asked.

Blade's stomach rumbled. "Ugh, yes."

"How about we find something to eat?"

He patted his flat belly. "I'm game."

They picked up their things and walked back to the bungalow a few steps away.

"This really is a prime location," Sophia said. "We have everything at our fingertips."

Especially you.

The thought popped into Blade's head before he could think straight. Once again, he had to remind himself that she was strictly a friend, nothing more. He'd promised the guys that he wouldn't take advantage of her.

The week stretched out in front of him. He wasn't sure he could keep that promise for an entire week. Not when they'd be spending so much time together.

As soon as they made it back to their room, Sophia ducked into the bathroom. Blade could hear the shower go on. While Sophia rinsed off, Blade got out his cellphone and dialed Mac's number.

"Miss me already?" Mac answered.

"Of course." As he stood in front of the sliding glass doors, gazing at the beach and water, he grinned. "I'm standing in our room, staring out at the water. The sun's shining and I've had my first Painkiller. Yeah, I'm missing you."

Mac laughed. "Why the call?"

"I need you to look up a name and see if you can find out anything on an Andrés Calderón."

"Why?" Mac asked.

"He hit on Sophia on the airplane and has asked her to join him at the *Cinco de Mayo* celebration in downtown Cancún. I want to see if he's legit, or if he's somebody I need to worry about."

"You're not letting her go with him, are you?"

"Of course not. I'm going with her. I'm just hesitant to go to downtown Cancún, off the resort, with Sophia."

"And rightly so," Mac said. "The cartels have been active in those areas. They usually don't bother tourists, but if you're in a non-tourist area, you do need to be careful."

"Exactly."

"Need us to come down and cover you and Sophia?" Mac asked.

"I wish. You guys would love it here. It's beautiful." *And so is Sophia,* he added beneath his breath. Why hadn't he noticed before? And now that he had, how could he un-notice it? She was his friend. She needed to stay his friend. He couldn't screw that up.

"I'll check on this Andrés Calderón and let you know."

"Thanks, buddy."

"And really, if you need us to come down and spot you..." Mac paused, "all you have to do is say the word."

"Thanks, man. I will." As Blade ended the call, the bathroom door opened.

Sophia stepped out in a bathrobe, her hair damp, her skin flushed a pretty peach color.

"Shower's all yours," she said. "I was going to do

my hair, but I don't think it's going to do any good. The humidity here will just keep it curling." A few drying tendrils curled around her face.

"I like the curls," he said.

She gave him a twisted smile. "Thanks."

He ducked into the bathroom carrying his shaving kit and an extra set of clothes. The room smelled like Sophia. A fragrant floral scent that tantalized him. He could imagine her standing beneath the shower spray rubbing scented bodywash all over her body. He found himself wishing that he'd done that.

"She's your friend," he muttered to himself as he turned the water to cool. Thinking otherwise would get him nowhere.

When Blade emerged from the bathroom, Sophia had dressed in a pretty, sunshine-yellow sundress and flat sandals. Curls were springing up all around her face, and she looked so bright and refreshing. Kissable. He found himself wanting to pull her into his arms.

And her smile lit up the place. Holy hell. She was just a friend, he repeated to himself.

Hell, he was in trouble.

CHAPTER 4

"GIVE me a few minutes to do my face and I'll be ready." Sophia slipped past Blade and into the bathroom.

"You don't have to go all out for me," he called out. "You already look great."

"You're so nice." Sophia gave him a patronizing smile. "But I'm not doing it for you."

Blade frowned. "You plan on flirting with someone else?"

She shrugged. "Maybe." She closed the door and went to work with her makeup.

A few minutes later, Sophia checked her reflection in the mirror one last time before stepping out of the bathroom. The soft yellow dress emphasized the green in her eyes. After several attempts with the straightener, she'd given up trying to control her riotous curls and fit a rhinestone encrusted comb in one side of her hair.

She'd added a little light makeup, including mascara, eyeliner and a soft coral-colored lipstick. She'd swapped the flat sandals for high heeled strappy sandals, wondering if she was making a mistake to wear them in a crowded celebration. However, the shoes looked so good, she hated not to wear them. For someone who wore jeans and T-shirts every day of the week, she actually felt beautiful in this, and she wondered what kind of reaction she'd get out of Blade.

She might not be beautiful, but she looked cute in the dress and cute might not be enough to grab Blade's attention, but she might grab Andrés Calderón's. One way or another she was going to have a good time that night. She'd prefer to dance with Blade, but if he wasn't asking, she'd definitely be dancing with Andrés. Tonight, she planned to dance.

When she stepped out of the bathroom, her breath caught in her throat. She stared across the room at Blade standing with his back to her, looking out the window at the ocean. He wore dark slacks and a white button-down shirt that contrasted beautifully with his black hair. As he turned toward her, his blue gaze captured hers.

His eyes widened. "Wow."

She smiled, her chest warming. "Wow, yourself."

"You look amazing."

Her cheeks heating, Sophia dipped her head. "Thank you. I guess we clean up pretty well for a couple from the Salty Dog Saloon."

"You'd look good no matter what you wear," he said. "But that dress is perfect on you."

Not used to compliments, Sophia's cheeks warmed. She imagined she was turning a bright red, and that was not an attractive color on her pale skin. "Are you ready?"

He nodded, his eyes narrowing. "Are you sure you want to go tonight? I'm still not convinced it's safe."

"Don't be such a worrywart," she said. "We're just going to go in town and enjoy a celebration, along with thousands of our closest friends." She grinned. "You don't have to go, you know."

"The hell I don't." His gaze raked her from top to bottom. "Especially when you're wearing that dress."

"I'm sure there will be much prettier girls, and no one will give me a second look."

"Sweetheart, that's where you're wrong. You're a novelty here in Mexico with that red hair and pale skin. You'll definitely stand out in the crowd." His brow lowered. "That's what's got me worried."

"I'll do my best to be careful," she said. "And I won't stray out of your sight."

"Damn right, you won't." He held out his elbow. "Are you ready?"

She nodded. "Let's go. I want to celebrate."

"You could do that here at the resort. I understand

that one of the clubs has good music and a program to celebrate *Cinco de Mayo*."

She nodded. "And we will enjoy the clubs in the resort another night. But tonight, we're going to join the locals in their celebration."

"Guess I'll have to find me a big stick to ward off all the horny bastards." He patted his chest. "I wish I had my gun."

"We'll be fine. And you'll be too busy fending off all of the women desperate to get to you. You won't even notice me."

He shook his head. "I'm on duty tonight. You're my top priority."

"What?" Sophia cocked an eyebrow. "You're not going to flirt with every skirt out there?"

Blade winked. "Not when the prettiest girl could be in danger."

They walked along the path to the hotel and entered through the back. They passed through to the front lobby and out to the driveway where a cab waited to take them into town.

Sophia had seriously debated staying at the resort and going to one of the night clubs there, but the entire idea was to make Blade jealous. Andrés's invitation gave Sophia the perfect opportunity for that. Besides, she also wanted the full experience of a true Mexican *Cinco De Mayo*.

Blade pulled his phone from his front pocket and checked the screen.

"Expecting a call?" Sophia asked.

"I was kind of hoping to hear from Mac," he said. "He was supposed to give me a call back."

Sophia's brow dipped. "Everything okay back home?"

He nodded. "Yes. I had a question for him. I had hoped he could answer before we left this evening."

"And what question was that?" she asked.

"Just a conversation I had with him earlier." He smiled. "Did I tell you that you smell good?"

Her eyes narrowed. "You're changing the subject."

He grinned. "Yes, ma'am. But you do smell good."

She shook her head with a slight smile.

"What kind of perfume are you wearing?" he persisted.

She snorted. "Just my bodywash."

"Well, it's nice."

The taxi driver got them as close as he could to the area where the celebration would take place. Already, there were so many people in the streets they couldn't drive any closer.

Blade paid the driver and helped Sophia out of the vehicle. Blade spoke Spanish to the driver and listened as the driver responded.

Once the cab left, Sophia looked up at Blade. "What did you say?"

He grinned. "I asked him where the cathedral was, and he pointed out that it was a couple of blocks ahead on the left. We just need to stay on this street.

He also said that in front of the cathedral was where all of the action would be with the food vendors, dancers and musicians."

Sophia's lips twisted. "I didn't know you could speak Spanish."

Blade puffed out his chest. "There's lots you don't know about me. I wouldn't say I speak fluent Spanish. I do know enough to get by. Things like how to order food and beer, and where's the bathroom."

Sophia chuckled. "The important things when visiting to Mexico."

"Exactly."

She hoped to get to know a lot more about him during the week they'd be together. In the meantime, she had a date with a handsome Mexican, with whom she hoped to make Blade jealous.

They hadn't even stepped out of the car when they could hear the music. And the closer they got to the city's center, the louder it grew. The locals wore colorful traditional costumes. Dancers in flowing, ruffled dresses swirled to the beat of the mariachi bands. Everybody was smiling and laughing.

An older gentleman with graying hair stepped in front of Sophia and held out his arms for her to dance. Sophia laughed and looked up at Blade.

Blade shrugged.

Sophia smiled at the older man and nodded.

With surprising agility, the man took her in his

arms and spun her around and then showed her how to salsa dance.

When the song ended, she laughed and thanked the man. "Gracias." When she returned to where Blade stood patiently waiting, Sophia was breathless but excited, her cheeks flushed with the heat. "That was fun." She looked up at Blade. "I don't suppose you know how to salsa, do you?"

His lips twisted. "Another thing you don't know about me."

She tilted her head to the side. "Well, do you?"

Another song started up. He took her hand in his and rested his other hand on her waist.

Since she'd had a lesson from the older gentleman, Sophia knew what to expect and moved in rhythm with Blade, her hips rocking, her feet keeping up with the music. The hand on her waist was warm. The music was hot. Before long, Sophia was hotter.

Blade twirled her away from him, and then back into his arms where she was crushed against his chest, their bodies moving together.

The song ended and another one followed immediately, this one slow and sexy. Blade held her close against him, resting his cheek against the side of her hair.

Sophia's hand rested on his heart. She could feel the beat thumping inside his chest.

When the song ended, they remained in each other's embrace. When a lively tune struck up,

Sophia tilted her head back and stared up into Blade's blue eyes. "Where did you learn to dance like that?"

He smiled. "Women love a man who can dance. I learned salsa from a pretty little *señorita* on a weekend trip to San Antonio."

His comment brought Sophia back to earth with a thud. She stepped out of his arms. "Well, she did good. I'm sure your next dance partner will enjoy your expertise. Right now, I need to make my way to the cathedral. It's almost eight o'clock."

"You're in luck," he said. "It's behind you."

Sophia spun to find a massive cathedral right behind her. She'd been so busy enjoying the music and dancing she hadn't noticed that they'd made it all the way to the cathedral. She was to meet Andrés Calderón. She wasn't that excited about meeting Calderón, but after Blade's comment about the pretty señorita who'd taught him to salsa, Sophia was ready to put her plan in place and attempt to make him jealous. She hoped her plan worked quickly, because her feet were starting to hurt. She was regretting the shoes she'd chosen.

"Ah, *Señorita Sophia. Buenas noches,*" a voice said from behind her.

She turned to find Andrés Calderón approaching her from the middle of the crowd. At first, she thought he was with a couple other men. They faded back amongst the revelers. "*Señor* Calderón." She dipped her head with a smile. "I'm glad you made it."

He held his arms wide. “I wouldn’t have missed it. I’ve looked forward to seeing the beautiful woman I met on the airplane again.” Calderón nodded toward Blade. “Thank you for bringing her. I will take good care of her.”

“I’m sure you will,” Blade said. His gaze turned toward Sophia. “Are you going to be all right?”

She nodded.

“Then I’ll be around,” he said. And he faded into the crowd.

Was he really going to leave her alone with Andrés? At that moment, she felt very alone in a crowd full of people. She spotted Blade standing to the side, leaning against a statue, his gaze fixed on her. He wasn’t even flirting with a woman at that point. Then a woman walked up to him, smiled, batted her lashes and flicked her skirt. He turned his attention and smiled down at the woman.

Heat built in Sophia’s cheeks. Well, two could play that game. She turned her smile up to Calderón. “I don’t suppose you can salsa?”

“*Si, señorita.*” Andrés swept her into his arms, moving her away from Blade and into the crowd of people dancing to the music.

He was good and had the natural grace of someone who’d been born to salsa. But it wasn’t the same as dancing with Blade. Still, she had fun. All the while they danced, she kept an eye on Blade as he stood talking with the pretty Mexican woman.

The more Sophia danced with her partner, the closer Calderón pulled her to him, his hand at the small of her back creeping downward toward her buttocks. A little alarmed, Sophia purposely moved his hand back up. Not taking the hint, his hands slipped down low again and cupped her buttocks.

"No, Andrés," she said firmly. "I don't like that."

He clutched her closer, holding her flush against his body. "It's okay. It's just a dance."

She shook her head. "That's not dancing. I don't like it. So, please stop."

He spun her away from him and back into his arms. His hands slipped down to her buttocks.

This time Sophia came to a complete stop. "I'm done dancing."

His brow furrowed. "You are done when I say you are done." He pulled her back into his arms.

She braced her hands on his chest and pushed, trying to get away from him.

Calderón held tight.

"Andrés, let go of me!" She struggled to break free of his grip.

Two men eased up beside them, moving closer than the crowd around them.

Sophia became aware of the danger too late.

Andrés attempted to pick her up.

Sophia kicked and fought, and nobody seemed to care. One of the men grabbed her feet, and she kicked him in the face. He swore and grabbed one leg while the other man grabbed the other. The music played on. Nobody stopped to stare or intervene.

Sophia was carried toward an alley. "Help!" she cried. As they entered the alley, Sophia screamed and fought, more desperate than before.

Then the men holding her loosened their grips, and she fell to the ground. She heard a hard crack.

Calderón spun away from her and fell to the ground. The men who had been holding her feet had let go and advanced on the man who'd attacked Calderón.

Sophia picked herself up off the ground and turned to find Blade standing in front of the two men moving toward him. Calderón staggered to his feet and headed toward Blade's backside. With his attention on the two men in front of him, Blade didn't see the man coming at him from behind.

Sophia searched the immediate area for a weapon and found a slat from a pallet, grabbed it and rolled to her feet. She went after Calderón, hitting him in the back of the head as he lunged toward Blade.

Blade was busy fending off the two big guys who had followed Calderón through the market square. He threw a sidekick into one guy's belly and punched the other one in the jaw, sending him flying backward. The two men came at him again and, like a whirlwind, he went after them, kicking and swinging, until both men crumpled to the ground, groaning.

Calderón rolled over onto his back, grabbed the board from Sophia's hands, and pushed her back with it. She fell on her backside and scrambled backward, trying to get to her feet.

"Leave her alone." Blade grabbed Calderón by the back of his shirt and swung him around.

"You shouldn't have interfered." Calderón lunged at Blade.

Blade was ready. He swung his fist, hitting Calderón in the nose. Blood flew everywhere. The man's eyes watered. He fell to his knees, clutching his face.

"Stay away from her," Blade glared at Calderón as he grabbed Sophia's hand and helped her to her feet. "You ready to go?"

She nodded and hurried away with Blade.

They stepped back into the crowd and mixed in with the others, working their way to the other side where the taxi had dropped them off. Once they were out of the thickness of the crowd, they looked around for a taxi, waved one down, climbed in and hurried back to the resort.

They didn't speak until they got back to the bungalow. Before they could discuss what had happened, Blade's cellphone rang. He answered it with, "Blade here."

Sophia watched as Blade's eyes narrowed.

"The cartel leader?" he said, his gaze going to Sophia.

Sophia's heart skipped several beats.

"*That* Calderón?" Blade pinched the bridge of his nose. "Great. All we needed was to have the entire drug cartel down on us."

Sophia sank to the sofa and waited for Blade to complete his call.

"We'll keep our eyes open, and we'll stick with the resort." When he ended the call, he stared across the room at Sophia, and her heart sank to her knees. "Do you want the good news or the bad news?"

"Is there any good news?" she asked.

"Umm, I'm afraid not. Your date tonight, the one whose nose I broke, happens to be the son of the local drug cartel's leader."

"I take it that's a bad thing. Nothing like being on the wrong side of a drug cartel. Should we pack up and leave now?" Sophia pushed to her feet. "I can be packed in just a few minutes."

Blade shook his head. "No. We'll wait and see. Hopefully, we just embarrassed him, and the dad won't take any actions against us. What's scary is that I suspect they were trying to kidnap you to sell in some human trafficking scheme."

Sophia nodded and shivered. "Otherwise, why would they have carried me off?"

"Exactly."

Sophia looked around the bungalow. "So, what do we do now?"

"Hunker down, and wait and see," he said. "We

should be all right here at the resort. They have sufficient security."

"What about our excursions that we'd planned? It seems a shame to be in Cancún and not see anything."

"The catamaran trip might be okay, as long as we do it last minute. Maybe, if we don't plan too far ahead, we can get out and about."

She sighed. "Every time we leave the resort, we put ourselves at risk."

"I'm not completely convinced that we're safe here at the resort. Especially out here in this bungalow. We might have been safer in the hotel tower." Blade patted his chest and side as if searching for something. "I wish I had a gun."

Sophia wrapped her arms around herself. "Is it that bad?"

"It could be. We'll just have to play it by ear," he said. "If it gets too bad, we'll leave."

Sophia nodded. "I guess that means we won't be taking a midnight stroll on the beach then." She gave him a trembling smile.

Blade shook his head. "Sorry. That puts you out in the open in the dark. We can't risk that."

Sophia shrugged. "That means there's nothing left to do but go to bed and hope we wake up in the morning."

Blade nodded. "You go ahead. I need to make some phone calls."

"This late at night?"

He nodded. "I really would like to have a gun."

"Wouldn't they throw you in jail if they catch you with one here in Mexico?"

"Have to catch me first. In the meantime, we need some protection."

"Okay then." She sighed. "I'm sorry I didn't realize who Calderón was."

"I think he was banking on that. A pretty, redheaded woman would sell high in the human trafficking market."

Sophia entered the bedroom, gathered up some clothes and carried them into the bathroom. She stripped out of the pretty dress, sad that it had been ruined in the fall. In the shower, she washed her hair and cleaned the makeup off of her face, and then scrubbed the street grime from her body. After she rinsed thoroughly, she climbed out and towel dried. Rather than slipping into her nightgown, she pulled on a pair of shorts and a T-shirt and exited the bathroom.

Blade had drawn the drapes over all the windows. He stood with his back to her, his body tense, his phone pressed to his ear. "Roger," he said into the phone, "I'll keep that in mind."

He hung up and turned to face her.

"Keep what in mind?" she asked,

"A contact who might be able to get me a gun."

Her brow furrowed. "If you're that worried, we need to leave."

"I'm just taking precautions." He reached out and brushed a damp strand of hair behind Sophia's ear. "We don't know that Calderón senior will do anything in revenge for me breaking his son's nose."

She cupped his hand and pressed it to her cheek. "How can I sleep when I'm worried?"

He kissed her forehead. "Go to bed. Close your eyes and, eventually, you'll go to sleep."

"What about you? I told you I'd sleep on the couch."

He shook his head. "I'm not having you sleep out here. I can sleep on the couch, and you in the bedroom. Leave the door open though." When she hesitated, he kissed her forehead again. "Just do it, Sophia."

She turned and entered the bedroom. Leaving the door open, she climbed into the bed. It didn't feel right going to bed when it was her fault they'd gotten into their current situation.

She'd bet money that Blade would be up all night.

Sophia lay for a long time staring up at the ceiling. She must have fallen asleep, because the next thing she knew she was in a dream being carried off by three men. She struggled and fought. Only this time, Blade wasn't there to protect her. She cried out his name. No one was there to help. Deep down, she knew it was a dream, but it felt so real, and she couldn't break free.

Then she felt strong arms wrap around her. For a moment she fought them until she heard a voice say, "It's okay. Sophia. It's me...Blade. You're okay. I've got you."

Sophia woke from her dream and looked up to see Blade's blue eyes staring down at her. "They had me again," she whispered.

"They don't have you now." He smoothed a hand over her hair. "I'm going to take care of you. Go to sleep, Sophia."

She rested her cheek against his chest and drifted back into a dreamless sleep. She was where she was meant to be.

CHAPTER 5

BLADE WOKE before Sophia the next morning. For a few long moments, he lay with her snuggled in his arms, her hand draped across his chest and her leg flung over his thigh. Her warm breath swept across his chest stirring the hairs there and awakening so much more.

Blade had never been one to lie in bed with a woman and not make love to her. This had to be a first.

The fact that Sophia was his friend made it even more difficult. Friends didn't make love to each other.

Yeah, right.

He'd heard of friends with benefits. But Sophia was better than that. She deserved a man who would treat her the right way. One who would love and protect her. Someone who would marry her and give her children.

Blade smiled as he imagined those children. Little redheaded hellions with the spunk and sass of their mother. Little girls with curly red locks, reaching up to their father with chubby little arms. "Pick me up, Daddy."

For the first time ever, Blade felt a tug of longing for a life he had never expected to want. Deltas didn't make good husband or father material, and he wasn't ready to give up his life as a Delta.

He needed to stick to the plan. He was there to protect Sophia, not to bed her.

But hell. She smelled so good, and she was so soft against him.

Blade felt his resistance crumbling.

Before the walls crashed down around him, he slipped from beneath her and rolled out of bed onto his feet.

Sophia stirred but didn't wake. Her freckled cheeks were flushed a pretty pale pink, and her lips were soft, full and begging to be kissed.

At least that's how Blade saw it, and he wanted to. He'd always been aware of Sophia, but only in a friend sense, not as anything else. He had been so conditioned to loving and leaving women that he couldn't see Sophia as a woman he would take to his bed.

Until now.

And it blew open a whole lot of doors that would be best left closed.

What would it be like to make love to Sophia? To have her pale skin lying naked on the bed next to his darker complexion? Her curly red hair spread out across a white pillow next to his, making a fan of coppery gold...?

He swallowed hard to keep a groan from rising up his throat. He wanted to crawl back into the bed with Sophia and awaken her with a kiss and more. Instead, he walked from the room and closed the door softly behind him. With every ounce of determination he could muster, he went to the small kitchenette where he brewed a cup of coffee, hoping that the caffeine and heat would quench the desire he felt for his friend and next-door neighbor. While the coffee brewed, Blade pulled back the curtains and let the morning sun into the bungalow.

He had to maintain focus. After what had happened the night before, he was afraid that Calderón's father and minions would soon be looking for them. He and Sophia would have to lay low for a couple days to make sure. That didn't mean that they couldn't go out to the beach. They would just have to stick to the resort and limit their outings to daylight. Maintaining situational awareness at all times was key to staying alive. Cartels weren't known to just strike at night. Some had gunned down people on the beach during the day. Hopefully, they could still enjoy their vacation just a little bit closer to the resort.

"Good morning," came a gravelly voice from behind him.

He turned.

Sophia stood in her T-shirt and shorts, her hair a tousled mane hanging down around her shoulders. She wiped the sleep from her eyes and blinked at the morning sun shining through the window. If she had been beautiful sleeping, she was even more striking standing there in an oversized T-shirt and shorts that did nothing to hide her sexy legs.

Blade took a gulp of his coffee, burned his tongue and sputtered.

Her mouth twisted into a wry grin. "Sorry, did I startle you?"

"No. Coffee's just a little hot," he said. If anything, he'd startled himself with the sudden surge of desire he wasn't quite able to tamp down. "You feel okay?" he asked.

She nodded. "After I finally got to sleep, I didn't have any more of those dreams." She gave him a weak smile. "Thank you."

He nodded. "No, thank you. At least I got a little bit of sleep on a real bed."

Her eyes narrowed. "And did you sleep?"

"I did."

"With one eye opened?"

He snorted. "Somewhat. But I feel rested, so I'm

okay. And it was a lot more comfortable in the bed than on the sofa, I have to admit. But don't worry. I'm okay with sleeping on the sofa tonight."

"We'll see," she said and padded barefoot toward the coffee pot. "Is there enough for me?"

"Plenty. As long as you like it hot, strong and black. If you want sugar and cream, we'll have to pick some up today."

She sniffed the air around the coffee pot and sighed. "No. I like it just this way."

He fished a mug out of a cabinet and set it on the counter next to the coffeemaker. He brushed her hand aside and said, "Here, let me pour. You're still sleepy."

She crossed her arms over her chest. "Thank you."

He filled her cup and set the carafe back in the coffeemaker.

She lifted the cup and leaned her back against the counter. "So, what have you decided?"

"About what?"

She captured his gaze over the rim of her cup. "Are we staying or going home?"

"I think we can stay and see how it plays out." Blade lifted his mug. "I might have a talk with the resort security team and let them know to be on the lookout for Calderón's thugs."

"Should we report the incident to the Mexican police?"

Blade shook his head. "No. If anything, they might

arrest me for having pummeled the local cartel leader's son. It might be best to just lie low."

Sophia frowned. "Does that mean we have to stay in this bungalow 24/7? Seems a shame to come all the way to Mexico to be stuck inside when the sun's shining and the surf's calling to us." She waved toward the beach and the morning sun rising over the water.

Blade smiled. "If we keep our wits about us, I think we can go out to the beach and some of the resort restaurants."

"That sounds good," Sophia said. "I wanted to relax anyway. If things work out and nobody attacks us, maybe we can do some of the excursions later on this week."

Blade nodded. "We'll see."

Her lips pressed together. "That almost sounds like a 'hell no'."

"Not so much a hell no as a probably not. But, like I said, we'll see. In the meantime, how would you like to get dressed and go find some breakfast?"

Sophia took a cautious sip of her coffee. "Sounds good. I'll only be a minute." She carried her coffee into the bedroom and closed the door behind her.

While Sophia changed, Blade rummaged through his duffle bag, found a nice polo shirt and pulled it over his head. Then he slipped into a pair of khaki shorts and sandals. It wasn't much of a bodyguard outfit, and he didn't have a weapon to protect them, but it would have to do. He made a note to buy a hat from the gift shop for a disguise. Then he settled a pair of sunglasses on his face and hoped that he would blend in with the tourist crowd until he could find a hat.

Moments later, Sophia emerged from the bedroom wearing a white eyelet sundress, a big floppy straw hat with her hair tucked up beneath it, and sunglasses. She couldn't hide her pale skin, but she'd done a good job of hiding her hair.

Blade grinned. "Good job."

She reached up to touch her hat. "Yeah, I thought it might be a good idea to hide my red hair."

He nodded. "You'd make a great spy."

Sophia laughed and shook her head. "I can hide the hair more easily than I can hide the pale tone of my skin. Makeup could never cover all the freckles."

"True. But from a distance, this will do." He held out his elbow. "Shall we?"

She hooked her arm through his. They left the rooms, securing the door behind them.

The walk up the path to the hotel was spent in silence. Blade searched every shadow and every face as they passed the other bungalows along the way. He saw no one but service staff and other guests of the resort. No one stared at him with menacing looks. He'd have to make a point to talk with the staff in charge of cleaning the bungalow. Maybe if he tipped them enough, they would lean toward protecting

Sophia and Blade, rather than giving up their location to the cartel. "When you were talking to Andrés, did you give him your full name?" Blade asked Sophia as they stepped into the hotel lobby.

She shook her head. "No, just my first name, Sophia."

"Well, that should slow him down a little bit."

"Do you really think he'll come looking for us?"

"I don't know. But it doesn't hurt to keep our eyes open. Promise me you won't go anywhere by yourself."

Sophia laughed. "Trust me, I won't." She squeezed his arm. "Thank you for coming and being my protector. I didn't realize I'd need you so much."

He glanced down at her and patted her hand. "I'm glad I'm here. Last night could've ended a whole lot worse."

Sophia nodded solemnly.

They found a small restaurant on the outskirts of the hotel with a view of the ocean. They settled beneath an umbrella that shaded them. Blade propped his menu in front of him and looked over the top, scanning the horizon and the people around them.

Sophia did the same, shooting a glance toward him. "See anybody we should be suspicious of?"

"Not so far."

She shook her head and clapped her menu shut.

"If we're going to have to hide everywhere we go, maybe it is best if we just go home."

"It's your call," he said. "But count on a hefty change fee for the flight."

Sophia grimaced. "It really makes me mad that one person can ruin my entire vacation."

"Vacation?" Blade's eyes widened. "He could've ruined your entire life."

Sophia nodded. "You're right. I should be grateful, but I'm really mad that he almost ruined my entire life." Her gaze connected with Blade's. "Do you really think he was kidnapping me to sell me into human trafficking?"

Blade shrugged. "Even if he was only kidnapping you for his own use, it wouldn't have been any better."

Sophia shook her head. "No, it wouldn't. I really hate to think that there are people in this world who do things like that. Why can't everybody be nice?"

"Not everybody is like you, Sophia."

"Wow, so you think I'm nice?" She grinned.

He winked. "For the most part."

Sophia's eyes narrowed. "What do you mean, for the most part?"

"I've seen you at work at the Salty Dog. You don't take crap off of anyone who steps over the line."

She tilted her head. "That's a bad thing?"

"Not at all. A woman needs to know how to protect herself. You do a pretty good job of that."

Her smile faded. "When it's three to one, what woman can defend herself from that?"

He shook his head. "That's why you never go any place like this by yourself, and even some places in the United States. Unfortunately, most women are smaller and weaker than men. It pays to be highly skilled in self-defense techniques. Otherwise, you're an easy target."

"Remind me to take self-defense classes when I get back."

Blade nodded. "That would be a good idea. I suggest Israeli Krav Maga."

Sophia nodded. "I've heard of that."

"In the meantime, stay close to me."

"You don't have to tell me twice."

They ordered their food and ate, talking about their mutual friends and plans each of them had for their own houses.

"I'd like to get a dog someday," Sophia said. "I'm thinking about building a fence in my backyard."

"I can help you with that," Blade offered.

She laughed. "When? You're almost never home."

Blade nodded. "Yeah, but when I am, I need something to keep me busy or I get into trouble."

"You do?" she asked, cocking an eyebrow.

"I know it's hard to imagine." Blade lifted his chin. "I was always in detention in high school. I made good grades, but I couldn't stand the pace. It was too slow."

"What about sports?"

"If I hadn't played on the football team, I doubt that the administration would have been as lenient on me. I'm sure they would've suspended my ass rather than give me detention, but they needed me because I was a pretty good receiver. They liked me because I scored."

"And you continue to score," she said with a smirk.

Blade nodded. "Touché. I deserve that. At least I always make sure the women I sleep with know, up front, that I'm not the marrying kind."

"I bet some still hold out hope that you'll change your mind."

His lip quirked up on one side. "There have been a few."

"I'm sure deep down, every one of those women you've slept with had high hopes of convincing you that they were the one."

His lips pressed into a thin line. "I'm not marriage material. I like being a Delta, and it's not conducive to long-term relationships."

"What about your buddies who've just gotten engaged?"

"It's extremely optimistic of them," he said.

"But you don't expect it to last, do you?" Sophia guessed.

"I don't see how it can. Once those guys are

deployed, the women are left behind. They have to handle everything. I mean, what if a pipe leaks?"

Sophia crossed her arms over her chest. "She can call a plumber."

"What if she gets sick?"

"Those ladies have a network of friends," Sophia said. "They'd come to her rescue."

Blade frowned. "But that's her partner's job."

"Those women know what they're getting into." Sophia shook her head. "It's their choice. If they didn't like the idea of their guys being deployed, they wouldn't have made the choice to stay with them. They're strong women. They can handle anything. After all, they were single before they met their guys."

"Exactly, and they'll be single again while their guys are deployed."

"Not exactly. They'll be really happy when their guys come home, and they can make up for lost time. Blade, you're not looking at the right women if you think all of them are going to bail on you. You need a woman who is strong, who can stand on her own, alone, and who will be there for you when you come home."

"Not all women are as strong as you are, Sophia." He reached across the table for her hand.

She laid hers in his.

If he was ever to fall for a woman and risk his heart and hers, it would have to be a woman like

Sophia. He'd seen her night after night at the Salty Dog Saloon.

She was strong, and she was smart.

The problem was that Blade wasn't the marrying kind.

"You're a good friend, Sophia." He squeezed her hand and let go. Reminding himself that she was a friend, not a life partner or lover. He didn't need to screw up his life or hers by getting too friendly with her. They had to live next door to each other. Maybe it hadn't been such a good idea to buy the house beside hers. But now that it was done, he needed to keep his distance.

He liked talking to her over the fence or sitting out in her garden. He'd hate it if that part of his life went away. And it would as soon as he slept with her.

When they finished their breakfast, they ducked into one of the shops where Blade bought a cap with Cancún written across the front of it. The cap covered his hair, making him look like any other tourist. Feeling a little better about his disguise, he suggested that they spend some time at the beach.

Sophia grinned. "I'm game."

They hurried back to the bungalow. All the while, Blade kept an eye out for anything or anybody unusual. When they arrived at their unit, he insisted on being the first through the door, checking the rooms before he allowed her to enter. When he was sure that it was clear, he let Sophia inside.

She insisted on being first in the bedroom to change into her swimsuit.

While she was changing, Maria, the maid, came by the room.

Between his rudimentary Spanish and the maid's limited English, Blade let her know that if anyone tried to get into their room while they were out, to let him know. She looked somewhat alarmed, and he explained to her about the incident that had happened the night before. If she'd looked alarmed before, she looked almost terrified when he finished.

Maria shook her head. "*No bueno, señor. No bueno.*"

"I know. That's why we're worried. So, can you keep an eye on things while we're gone?"

She nodded. "*Si, señor.* I will let you know."

"And if you know anybody who knows of the cartel's movements," he added, "I'd love to talk to them."

Maria appeared to be a woman who didn't much care for the local cartel. She crossed herself like a good Catholic. "I have a cousin," she said, "I will let him know."

"Thank you, Maria."

She nodded. "You and the *señorita* be safe. I will return when you have left the room."

He smiled at the housekeeper. "Gracias, Maria."

When Maria left, the door to the bedroom opened.

"Did I hear you talking to someone?" Sophia

stood in the doorway, wearing her royal blue bikini and lightweight cover-up. She looked absolutely beautiful.

Blade's heart skipped several beats before he could answer her question. "I was talking to Maria, the cleaning lady. She'll come back to take care of the room after we've left."

"Did you warn her to be careful coming in and out in case somebody tries to get into our room?"

He nodded. "I did warn her. She's aware of who Calderón is."

"Great," Sophia said. "I'm the only one in Mexico who didn't."

"I don't think most people coming here look up cartel names. Tourists just assume everything will be all right."

"Still, you hear too often about women who are kidnapped from resorts. They either never find them or find their bodies after it's too late. You'd think I would be smart enough not to get myself in a situation like that."

"You couldn't have known," Blade said.

"Anyway, I'm glad you informed her," Sophia said. "I would hate to see her get hurt because of us."

"Exactly."

Sophia frowned. "Are you sure it's okay for us to go out?"

"I hate to be held hostage by anybody," Blade said,

his brow furrowing. "If we remain indoors, we're being held hostage. And maybe for no reason at all."

"Exactly how I feel." Sophia snagged a towel and her sunscreen, and then plunked a hat on her head where her hair was still drawn up into a tight knot. "Let's go."

They spent the day on lounge chairs, hiding under an umbrella and watching the surf. Sophia faced toward the ocean while Blade turned toward the resort. That way they had both directions covered, and it gave Blade all too much time to study the freckles on Sophia's face, neck, shoulders, and the tops of her breasts.

When she asked him to smear sunscreen on her shoulders and back, he almost declined, knowing how it would feel and the reaction his body would have. But if he declined to perform the task, he would have to explain, and he wasn't ready for that.

Sophia didn't need to know that he was lusting after her body.

With a fake smile, he nodded and said, "Sure." As soon as he had the sunscreen smeared on her, he excused himself and dove into the water. He didn't stay under long. He had to keep an eye on Sophia. Thankfully, she followed him out to the water, which made watching her easier.

Once she was in the water and her hair was wet, it looked as dark as anybody else's, not the glorious strawberry-blond that was so unique and recognizable.

She dove into the water, grabbed his ankle and pulled. He went under, grabbed her around the waist, picked her up and threw her into the surf. Then he dove in to tickle her. They both came up from the water sputtering and laughing.

"I can see why all the guys love you," Blade said.

Sophia laughed. "Hah. You know how many dates I've gone on in the last six months? I can't even count them on one hand because there weren't any. So, I don't know why you think all the guys love me."

Blade smiled. "You should've heard the talking to I got from the guys when I told them I was taking you to Cancún."

"Oh, yeah?" Sophia's eyebrows rose. "What did they say?"

"They told me not to break your heart. That they like seeing you at the Salty Dog. You're one of their favorite people. They were afraid I'd screw things up."

Her eyelids drifted low. "And will you?"

For a moment he hesitated. The way her eyelids drooped, and her lips puffed out made Blade's groin tighten. The urge to pull her into his arms and crush her lips with his was so powerful, he nearly caved into his desire. Instead of grabbing her and yanking her into his arms, he planted his hands on top of her head and dunked her under the water.

Once again, she dove for his ankles and pulled him off his feet. Then she pounced on his chest and drove him down into the water until his back hit the sand. He grabbed her around the waist and held on. She was staring at him through the water, her eyes wide open.

His resistance was futile. He leaned up and captured her lips with his in a salty wet kiss. Together they bobbed to the surface. When the sun struck him, he realized what he'd done, and he broke away from her and planted his feet in the sand. Waves washed up to his waist.

"I shouldn't have done that," he said.

She met his gaze straight on. "But you did, and you can't take it back."

"No," he said, "but I won't do it again."

Her lips curled into a sultry smile. "No?"

His eyes narrowed. "No. Friends don't kiss friends."

"Friends with benefits do. Have you ever thought of that kind of arrangement?" she asked, tilting her chin. "I know I have."

His groin tightened even more. Hell, he'd slept in the same bed with her the night before, and it had been all he could do to keep from taking her. It had been a long hard night. If he hadn't been so tired, he wouldn't have slept at all. And it looked like he was going to have another long hard night trapped in the same bungalow with the red-haired beauty.

He still couldn't understand why Sophia didn't think of herself as beautiful. She was. A more unique beauty he'd never met. Each freckle on her face, shoulders and arms told a story of a strong woman with a big heart and an infectious laugh. Every time it rang out at the Salty Dog, heads turned. It was only a matter of time before some lucky fool married her.

That thought didn't sit well with Blade. He couldn't imagine her with anyone except himself. Then he remembered where he was, and he searched the beach and the ocean for the enemy. The woman made him lose focus, and that was a dangerous place to be if the cartel decided to even up the score. They could strike at any time. "Come on, let's get back under the umbrella. I feel a little safer in the shadows."

"I feel a little safer in the shadows, too. My skin won't get burned as quickly, and you can apply more sunscreen on it." She gave him an innocent smile.

He frowned. "You're on your own there."

She shook her head. "But you're my protector. I need you to help protect my skin from the sun." She raised her eyebrows. "And I can't get my back. Do you want me to ask a complete stranger to do the honors?"

"Hell no," he replied, gruffly. "Maybe it's time to go back to the bungalow."

"What? And miss this beautiful ocean breeze? No,

I don't think so," Sophia said. "However, I could do with another drink. Think we could snag a waiter?"

As they approached their lounge chairs and umbrella, they spotted a waiter at another set of chairs and flagged him down. They spent the next hour sitting beneath the umbrella, drinking Mai Tais and enjoying the breeze.

It was easy to forget that they might have a cartel after them with the salty scent of the beach filling the air and the sun shining down on them. Maybe he was worrying too much. Still, he couldn't let his guard down.

When they returned to the bungalow, Sophia curled up in one of the chairs with a book and promptly fell asleep. The room had been cleaned. Maria had been there, leaving a chocolate on their pillows and fresh towels in the bathroom.

Blade would have carried Sophia to her bed, but that would mean touching her body. At the moment, he didn't feel like he could touch her without wanting to kiss her again. He left her curled up in the chair and spent the time studying her every feature, realizing with every passing minute how much deeper he was getting. How wrong would it be to fall in love with his next-door neighbor?

SOPHIA MUST HAVE FALLEN asleep reading her book. When she awoke, the shadows in the room had lengthened, and the sun was on its way down. Her stomach rumbled.

"Hungry?" a voice asked.

She looked up and stretched.

Blade stood in the kitchenette, his hands curled around a mug of what smelled like coffee.

"I am hungry," she said. "What do you want to do for dinner?"

"They have a nice steakhouse here on the resort. I called and made a reservation. You have exactly one hour to get ready. Then I'm taking you dancing at the bar, which is also here on the resort."

She yawned and stretched. "So, you're telling me I should probably dress nicely, that I can't go in my swimsuit."

Blade smiled. "I wouldn't mind, but there might be a dress code."

Despite the threat of a drug cartel being after them, Sophia had enjoyed an exciting, pleasurable day with Blade in the sun and in the water. Especially in the water with that unexpected kiss.

CHAPTER 6

BLADE STOOD BEFORE SOPHIA, dressed in tailored black slacks, a white button-down shirt, a red necktie and a black fitted jacket.

Sophia's breath caught.

Sweet Jesus. The man was drop dead gorgeous.

Sophia had dressed in a shimmering white dress that reached her ankles, with a low V-neck and a scooped back that exposed skin all the way down to curve of her buttocks. Beth had chosen the dress for her. Around her neck, she wore a simple gold chain with a solitary diamond her mother had left her.

She'd felt beautiful when she'd looked in the mirror. But now as she stood there staring at Blade, who looked better than any of the actors in a James Bond movie, she worried that she didn't look good enough.

Then she noticed the hungry expression on his face.

"Wow," he said. "You look amazing."

Heat filled her cheeks. "You don't look so bad yourself."

"Who would have thought two blue-jean-clad regulars at the Salty Dog Saloon could look this good?"

She laughed. "Sarge would be proud. He's like a father to me. He and my dad were in the Marines together. I don't know what I would've done if Sarge hadn't been around when my folks drowned in Canyon Lake."

"What happened to them?"

"They were out fishing when the wind got a little bit rough. The boat capsized. Neither one of them had their life jacket on. They were too far from shore to swim in, and the wind caused pretty hefty waves. The authorities found the boat. A couple days later, they found Mom and Dad. I was in college when I got the call, finishing my final semester. I missed a couple of weeks and almost didn't pass my end of semester exams. It didn't seem right going back to school after they passed." Sophia shook her head. "Actually, nothing seemed right. I got my degree in accounting. I passed the CPA exam, but accounting reminded me of Mom and Dad. That's what they'd wanted me to do."

"What a blow," Blade said. "It must've been hard."

Sophia nodded. "Sarge came to my graduation. He offered me a position at his bar. I agreed just so I could be close to somebody I knew. I felt so alone. I lived with him for a while, and then I moved into an apartment over the bar. I saved all of my tip money, which was pretty good, and made a down payment on a house. That's when I moved out of the apartment over the bar."

"So, you don't use your accounting degree?"

She shook her head. "On the contrary, I do. The first quarter of every year, I volunteer to help people with their taxes—people who can't afford an accountant. I figured my mom and dad would have wanted me to."

"They probably would've wanted you to put your accounting degree to work and get paid for it."

She nodded. "And I will...someday. But I like working at the Salty Dog. I like the people I've met, and I love Sarge. I really didn't get to know him until I worked with him. He's one of the best humans I've ever met."

Blade nodded. "I've known him to loan money to young soldiers when they didn't have enough to get home for Christmas."

Sophia nodded with a smile. "That sounds like Sarge. He'd give the shirt off his back to whomever needed it. I'm a prime example. But enough about me. What about you?" She tipped her head toward his outfit, her gaze running over him from head to toe. "How'd you learn to dress so nicely? I thought a lot of the guys in the military only knew how to wear their uniforms."

He laughed. "It's true. For most of them, that's all they know."

She smiled. "That suit looks tailored."

He nodded. "My family had money."

Sophia's eyes narrowed. "Then why the Army?"

"If I had wanted to, I could've stepped into my family's wealth, but I didn't because then I would've had to do things my father's way. My father and I are too much alike. We butt heads all the time. I couldn't stay. I had to make my own way on my own terms."

"So is the suit a relic of your high school days?"

"Well, no. I bought the suit. My pay isn't great as a soldier in the Army, but I do manage my money, and I've invested well. I can afford a nice suit. I just happened to need one when my mother died. I didn't make it back for the funeral, so I visited her graveside dressed as I would have, had I made it home in time."

Tears rose in Sophia's eyes. "I'm sorry."

"You and me both. I was deployed when she died." He looked away. "I didn't get to say goodbye to her. I wasn't there as she passed. It was bittersweet. She was a good woman, loved by so many."

"I know what you mean. My mom and dad had closed caskets. I didn't even get to see them one last time. At least I got to go to their funeral, so I did have a little bit of closure."

"I was on a mission. I couldn't get back until after the funeral. I hadn't talked to my mother in three months before she died. I didn't even know she was sick. She had a fast-moving cancer. It was only six weeks from the time they diagnosed it until the time she died. She didn't want my father to notify me, knowing that I was deployed. Too often we were out in the field with no internet access. But I would have made time. I could have found some way to contact her, and I wish I had."

Sophia closed the distance between them and laid her hand on his arm. "You can't undo the past, and you can't live the rest of your life beating yourself up. Your mother wouldn't have wanted that."

He nodded. "I know." He drew in a deep breath and let it out, forcing a smile to his lips. "Enough depressing talk. We're in Cancún on vacation. Let's have some fun tonight."

Sophia smiled to match his. "I'm in." She hooked her arm through his, and they stepped out the door. The sun had set, but there was still some lingering light in the sky. The path was lit with lights aimed up into the palm trees.

As they hurried toward the resort hotel, Blade kept his eyes on everything around them while Sophia scanned the shadows.

She hated that she didn't feel safe. At any moment, somebody could jump out and attack them. She was glad Blade was with her. She might not be able to fight off anybody, but Blade sure had a knack for it, as he'd proven.

Several times when the wind blew the palm fronds, the shadows shifted. Sophia jumped, wishing she had that board she'd used the night before to hit Calderón in the head. She might not have been able to defend herself, but she had been able to help Blade when it was three against one. She'd do it all again.

Hopefully tonight, she wouldn't have to.

Blade led the way through the resort to the steakhouse where the maître d' met them at the podium and led them to their seats. Their table was located near the rear of the room, where Blade sat with his back against the wall. They both ordered filet mignon with a side of baked potato and sauteed asparagus.

Blade chose a red wine to go with the meal and it was perfect. Everything was perfect. Throughout the meal, they talked about sports and their favorite football teams.

"I can't believe you live in Texas and your favorite team is not the Dallas Cowboys," Blade said.

"I prefer college football more than the NFL, but if you're talking the NFL, I'm all for the Denver Broncos."

"Why the Broncos?"

She laughed. "I like their mascot. I've always wanted a horse."

"That's the only reason?"

"And their colors. The colors are cool." She grinned. "But I admit I do root for the Cowboys when they aren't playing the Broncos."

Blade leaned back in his chair. "What about college football?"

"I always root for the Aggies," she said. "But I also like to watch Alabama play. What about you? And it's a tough choice when the service academies are playing. I usually root for Army."

Blade nodded. "You're in luck. I'm an Aggies fan. A couple of my favorite commanders were Aggies. I figured if they were good enough to put out a good leader, they were worth rooting for. And you can't go wrong cheering for Army."

"Okay, here's a good question," Sophia started. "You're so against marriage, have you ever been married?"

Blade blinked a couple times. "Okay, that's a little bit off the topic of sports."

Sophia leaned back. "Not that I'm interested. I'm just curious."

"Besides the fact that I'm Delta Force, I watched my parents during their miserable marriage." He lifted his wine glass and stared at it rather than into Sophia's eyes. "They stayed married even though they didn't really love each other. They argued a lot. It didn't make me want to commit matrimony."

Sophia laughed. "Commit matrimony? Is that like committing murder?"

His lips quirked up at the corners. "Sometimes, it felt like it between my parents."

"You know it's not always that way," Sophia said. "My parents were happily married. They loved each other until the day they died."

He looked across the table into her eyes. "Then you were lucky."

"Yes, I was," she said.

Blade set his empty wine glass on the table and looked around for the waiter. "Are you still hungry? Do you want some dessert?"

Sophia shook her head. "I'm so full. The meal was excellent."

Blade let the waiter know they were finished. A few minutes later, the waiter was back with the bill.

"Let me pay for my half," Sophia said.

"No way," Blade said, shaking his head. "You gave me a free ride down here and free lodging. The least I can do is pay for a meal."

"Yeah, but I won that free ride. It's not coming out of my pocket." She lifted her chin. "Besides, we're friends, and friends split the bill."

"You're right. We are friends. But this time, I'm going to pull rank on you, because if I'd known you'd insist on splitting the bill, I would've gone to a place that wasn't as expensive."

Sophia grimaced. "That much?" Sophia reached across the table for the bill. "Let me see."

He held the check away from her. "No, just trust me. I'll get it this time."

Sophia frowned. "Then I'm getting the next meal."

"Whatever." Blade opened his wallet and laid a couple of one-hundred-dollar bills in the folder with the bill.

Sophia's stomach clenched. That was a lot of money. At least a couple night's worth of tips. "Promise me we won't eat somewhere this expensive again."

He nodded. "Okay, but it was nice to celebrate one night."

She nodded. "Thank you."

He stood and held her chair while she rose to her feet. "By the way, you look stunning in that dress."

Sophia chuckled. "I think you said that already but thank you again."

"I can't wait to see it shimmering in the disco light."

"Disco?" She met his gaze. "Really?"

He laughed. "It's disco night at the bar with the dance floor."

"You're kidding, right?"

He laughed. "Yes, I am. They have a bar that caters to classical music or big band era music. I thought we'd start there. And then if you feel like it, we can go to the disco bar."

"Sounds good," she said with a smile. Then her brow dipped. "Only now, I'm a little intimidated."

"Intimidated?" Blade's head tilted. "Why?"

"You've already proven that you can salsa dance. You were raised in an affluent home. I can only imagine that you know all the dances." She stared up into his blue eyes. "Am I right?"

He shrugged. "Maybe."

"Well, at least tell me you know them well enough to lead somebody who doesn't know any of them."

He smiled confidently. "We'll manage."

"Now, I'm really intimidated." Sophia chewed on her bottom lip.

"Relax. We'll have fun." Instead of offering his arm, he took her hand and held it all the way through the winding halls of the resort to the bar where a band had set up. They played classic songs from the nineteen-forties and fifties.

True to his word, Blade made certain Sophia had fun. He led her through the dances like a professional. She learned how to do the fox trot and the swing. Fortunately, she already knew how to waltz; she'd learned that on a country and western dance floor.

It was like living a fairytale, dancing in Blade's arms. The way he looked, the way he danced, the way he treated her, he could have been a prince. After several sets the band took a break.

"Thank goodness," Sophia said. "My feet were beginning to hurt."

"Are your shoes not comfortable?"

She laughed. "Anything with heels is uncomfortable, but they look good."

"You could kick them off and dance barefoot," he suggested.

She nodded. "And I might, but I'm not sure how sticky the floor is. If it were the Salty Dog, I'm sure it would be layered with spilled beer. And the thought of dancing on sticky beer isn't something I relish."

He nodded. "Can't blame you there."

After they found seats, a waiter came by and took their orders for fresh drinks. Sophia ordered a glass of red wine, Blade a whiskey on the rocks.

As he settled back and waited for the drinks to appear, Blade nodded toward a point over her shoulder. "Turn your head slowly."

Sophia frowned. "Why?"

"Just do it…slowly."

Sophia turned as directed.

"See that man standing there in the far corner?" Blade asked, his voice soft and low so only she could hear.

Sophia noted a man wearing a white guayabera shirt.

He leaned against the wall, his arms crossed over his thick chest.

"What about him?" Sophia returned her attention to her table.

Blade lifted his glass and tossed back the

remainder of his cocktail. "He came in shortly after we did, and he's been there the entire time."

Sophia's lips pursed. "Could he be a bouncer?"

Blade glanced around the room filled mostly with an older crowd. "I doubt they have much need for a bouncer in this bar. Maybe in the disco bar they might. I gave him the benefit of the doubt…until the other one showed up."

Sophia's eyes widened. "What other one?"

He tilted his head to the left. "Other corner."

Sophia spotted a man standing in the shadowy corner to the left of the other one. He wore a black T-shirt. Barrel-chested, the man had heavy black eyebrows and probably ate nails for breakfast. And he was looking directly at them. As soon as Sophia spotted him, his gaze shifted to where the band had vacated the stage.

"Okay," Sophia said. "Now, you've got me spooked."

"I didn't mean to worry you. I just wanted you to be aware. I've had my eye on them all evening. We might take a different route back to the bungalow."

"Like maybe the one past hotel security?" Sophia suggested.

He smiled. "Yes. Hopefully, the security personnel are for more than just show."

Sophia glanced again at the two men standing guard in the corners. "Maybe these guys are part of that security team."

"We can ask on our way through," Blade said. "Do you want to stay for another set?"

Sophia shook her head. "No. I've had enough for tonight. After playing out in the sun all day, I am pretty tired."

They sat for a while longer and drank the drinks that the waiter brought. When they were finished, they stood. Sophia reached for Blade's hand. He held it in a firm grip as he led her through the maze of corridors zig-zagging through the resort. At one point he climbed stairs they didn't need to climb, just to break it up. They came back down in an elevator that brought them out to the lobby where the security guard sat at the front desk with the receptionist and clerks.

Blade approached the guard and spoke to him in Spanish. The man shook his head, and Blade nodded. "Gracias." Blade led them toward the door that would take them out to the walkway that led to their bungalow.

The security guard left his desk and followed them.

"Why is he following us?" Sophia asked beneath her breath.

"I asked him to," Blade said. "He said that they don't station bouncers in that particular lounge."

Sophia's brow wrinkled. "If they were working for Calderón, why didn't they make a move while we were dancing?"

"I don't know, and I still can't be certain that they're working for Calderón."

"What about the security guard? Do you think that he could be in with drug cartel?"

"I don't think so. I mentioned Maria." Blade grinned. "He said that she was his cousin, and he'd heard about our situation."

They made it all the way back to their bungalow without incident, though Sophia jumped at every shifting shadow. There were a lot because the breeze tossed the palm trees overhead and the lights pointed up at them danced.

The security guard opened their door for them and went inside first. When he came out, he gave a nod. *"Buenas noches, señor y señorita."*

"Gracias," Sophia said.

After the guard left, Blade led Sophia into the bungalow. The lights were all on. Blade locked the door and pulled the curtains closed. Then he performed his own inspection of the premises. When he came out of the bedroom and bathroom area, he nodded. "All clear."

"Good." Sophia kicked off her heels. "I hated the thought of having to run in these."

"You could have worn tennis shoes with your outfit."

She laughed. "Hah! No way. Beth would never forgive me. She helped me choose the dress."

"You both did good." His gaze swept over her. "It was worth whatever you spent on it."

Her cheeks warmed, the heat spreading throughout her body and coiling at her core. "Thank you again. It was a wonderful evening. I could almost forget for a few moments that we may be targeted by a drug cartel. All in all, it was a beautiful day. I enjoyed it thoroughly."

"And so did I," Blade said with a smile. "Would you like a drink before bed?"

"Do we *have* anything to drink?"

Blade chuckled. "I had Maria stock the refrigerator with beer and wine, and I also had her bring in a bottle of whiskey. I had to guess at what kind of wine you might like. Fortunately, it's red like you drank at dinner tonight."

"Then yes, I would like a glass of wine. Let me get out of this dress. Feels like overkill in this bungalow." She hurried into the bedroom, slipped the straps of her dress off her shoulders, and let it fall to her feet.

She'd worn nothing but a pair of thong panties beneath. What would Blade think if she walked out in nothing but her thong and her high heels? It would be worth putting those heels back on just to see his reaction. For a moment she considered doing that, and then she remembered how he'd reacted after he'd kissed her. She didn't want him to feel uncomfortable if she forced herself on him.

Sophia slipped a T-shirt over her head and pulled

on a pair of soft, jersey shorts. She entered the bathroom, grabbed a brush and considered running it through her wild curls. Knowing it would be fruitless, she laid the brush on the counter and pulled her hair up into a ponytail on top of her head.

No. Just no. It made her look like a twelve-year-old.

The last thing she wanted was to look like a twelve-year-old in front of Blade. It was bad enough wearing a T-shirt and shorts. She didn't have the nerve to wear the baby doll nightgown Beth had helped her pack. Maybe, just maybe, by the time they left, she'd have the nerve to wear it in front of him.

If the kiss was any indication, he wasn't completely immune to her. She had six more days to break down those walls. But tonight, she'd just get comfortable with him.

Sophia finger-combed her hair in an attempt to fluff the curls into some semblance of order. Finally, she gave up.

Sophia shot one more glance in the mirror before she left the bathroom. Tomorrow night, she would take the time to straighten her hair. Or not. The humidity in Cancún would keep her hair frizzy. So, for tonight, it was curls. How sexy could a woman be with a red, curly head of hair and freckles over just about every inch of her body? It was just as well that she was wearing her T-shirt and shorts. It wasn't like she was anywhere close to being a vamp. She chuckled as she wondered if anybody ever used that word anymore. She was still smiling as she left the bathroom and bedroom.

"What's so funny?" Blade asked handing her a glass of wine.

"Nothing," she said, "Everything. From curly red hair to cartel members in guayabera shirts. When things seem rough, you just have to laugh."

He gave her a quizzical smile. "I'm not quite sure how curls and cartels are connected, but I'm sure there's something that ties them together."

She touched a hand to her hair. "They're the bane of my existence at this point."

After handing her a wine glass, Blade reached out to touch one of her curls. "I happen to like your curls. You don't wear it like this at the bar."

She smiled. "It's dry enough in Texas, I can use a straightening iron to keep the curls at bay. The humidity here keeps me from straightening it. I just have to let the curls go."

He rolled one of the curls around his fingers. "I'm glad you did. I get to see a very different side of you, at least where your hair's concerned. I like it."

Once again, her body warmed from the point where he touched her hair all the way to her core. "If you keep saying nice things, I might begin to think that you like me." She touched the glass to her lips and looked over the rim into his eyes.

"Well, there's no doubt in my mind that I like you.

You're the best waitress and bartender at the Salty Dog Saloon, and you hooked me up with my house. You're also an awesome neighbor. The fact that you like to drink beer and watch football makes you even more amazing."

"Like one of the guys?" she asked, wrinkling her nose.

"Better. You have bright, coppery hair."

She shook her head and drank a long drink of her wine.

"None of my guy friends have pretty red curls." He winked.

The way he touched her hair, made her want to lean into his hand. Sophia had to step away or she'd make a fool of herself. "It's too bad we can't take a walk on the beach in the moonlight." Sophia turned away and strode into the living room, pacing the length of it.

"If nothing happens within the next day or so, we might consider doing that before we leave," Blade said from behind her.

She spun toward him. "I'd like that. I haven't walked on the beach in the moonlight since I was a teenager down at South Padre. I imagine it's quite a bit different here in Cancún."

Blade sat on the sofa and patted the seat beside him. "Come sit down. Those feet have to be killing you."

Part of her wanted to take that seat beside him

and try to convince him that she was more than just a friend. The other part of her was almost afraid to sit beside him and get her hopes up.

That first part of her won. She settled on the sofa beside Blade. How was she going to make him see her as anything other than a friend, unless she pushed the envelope?

CHAPTER 7

AS SOON AS Sophia sat down beside him, Blade realized his mistake.

Already having a tough time of maintaining the line between friends and lovers, having her beside him in her short shorts and T-shirt, with no bra beneath it, was tempting fate. What he needed was a willing woman to take to bed to slake his desires, but he couldn't imagine any other woman than the one he was with.

Curious about her freckles, Blade wondered if the soft dots of color were everywhere on her body? How he'd like to explore and find out.

He closed his eyes. No, he wasn't there to explore Sophia's body. He was there to protect it. Blade needed to remind himself of that more and more every day. The woman had no idea how tempting she was.

He downed his glass of whiskey and considered getting up to get another, but over the course of the evening, he had already had three and that was plenty, even with the food they'd eaten. Any more alcohol would dull his senses. And that night he'd be sleeping again with one eye open. Thankfully, he was a light sleeper, and sleep would be even harder to come by because he planned on doing it on the couch that night. He didn't dare sleep with Sophia. It was too hard. He was too hard. Every time she moved, every time she touched him, she stole his breath away. She made him want to crush her to him and kiss her.

He figured if the two guys in the bar were truly cartel thugs, they might make their move at night. They could be spying on them, waiting to inform the cartel of Sophia and Blade's whereabouts. In which case, they could have followed them and the hotel guard all the way to the bungalow.

Blade had half a mind to sleep on the floor that night and convince Sophia to do the same. Cartels had automatic weapons. If they decided to unload on the bungalow, it wouldn't take long before a bullet hit one of them.

The security guard had confirmed that there was a security camera on the corner of the bungalow and along the pathway leading from the hotel to the bungalows. He would keep an eye on the cameras and warn them if anyone was coming their way. But what if they came in from the ocean? The security guard wouldn't see it until they were right there at the bungalow.

Sophia finished her glass of wine and set the glass on the table. She leaned back on the sofa and closed her eyes.

"Tired?" he asked.

She nodded. "Yes, I could go to sleep right here."

"Why don't you go on to bed?"

"That would require me getting up," she said with a sigh. "I don't think I can do that right now."

The problem with Sophia falling asleep on the couch was that Blade was going to sleep there. And he'd promised himself that he wouldn't sleep with Sophia that night. He hated to disturb her, so he let her rest there.

Her eyes being closed gave him the opportunity to study her face. She'd cleaned off any makeup. He could see that her eyelashes were the same pretty red as her hair. The soft freckles across her cheeks were even more pronounced after spending the day in the sun. Her lips appeared soft and beautiful, just like her, and he was sorely tempted to taste them.

No, it wouldn't do for Sophia to fall asleep next to him. The longer she sat there and the deeper her breaths became, the hotter he got. If he wasn't so worried about her safety, he'd go out and find a woman to take to bed, but the thought of anyone else just didn't appeal to him. Abruptly, he rose from the couch, afraid if he sat there much longer, he wouldn't be able to get up.

Sophia blinked her eyes open. "Where ya going?"

"Nowhere, but you're going to bed." He held out his hand, and she laid hers in his. He pulled her to her feet then scooped her legs out from under her and carried her into the bedroom.

"You know you don't have to carry me," Sophia murmured, her breath warm on his neck. "I can walk on my own."

"You're tired," he reasoned.

She looped an arm around his neck and held on until he stood beside the bed. "You know you don't have to sleep on that couch tonight."

He laughed. "Yes, I do."

"It's not long enough for you. You're so tall. You could've left me on the couch and slept in here."

He shook his head. "No, this bedroom is the most fortified of all of the rooms. If somebody breaks in, they're going to go through the door or one of the large patio doors. It's best if I stay out there, and you stay in here." He laid her down on the bed.

She didn't unloop her arm from around his neck right away. Instead, she stared up into his eyes. "What if I have a dream again?"

"I'm in the next room. All you have to do is call out."

"Promise?"

He nodded and pressed a kiss to her forehead. "I promise."

Sophia tightened her hold around his neck and pulled him down to her, pressing her lips to his.

He returned the pressure before he could think straight.

When she opened to him, he swept his tongue in to caress hers. His body tightened. His pulse quickened. If he didn't leave soon, he wouldn't. He reached around his neck and loosened her grip, squeezed her hands and laid them beside her on the bed. Then he leaned back and said, "I swore we wouldn't do this."

"It's not nice to swear," she said and smiled. Her shirt had bunched up some and exposed her midriff.

"Sweetheart," he said, his voice tight, "I don't want to ruin a perfectly good friendship."

She stared up at him with her deep green eyes. "What if I don't want to be your friend?"

He was so very tempted. "That would be a real shame. I would miss you as a friend. Go to sleep, Sophia."

"What if I have a bad dream?"

"Leave the door open. I'll hear you."

Disappointed, she laid back against the pillow and stared up at the ceiling. "Goodnight, Blade," she said, her tone curt.

Blade left the room before he decided to stay.

. . .

Sophia's gaze followed him through the door. Well, hell, so much for seducing the man. He really was determined to stay in the "friend zone."

The lights blinked out in the living room and silence descended.

She couldn't even open a window to let the sound of the waves lull her to sleep. Sophia could hear the sound of ice clinking against glass.

Blade was just as awake as she was, only he had the advantage of a drink in his hand.

"Blade?" she called out softly.

"Yes, Sophia?"

"Have you ever been in love?" she asked softly.

For a long moment he didn't answer. "I thought I was once."

She scooted up into a sitting position. "Really? What happened?"

He snorted. "When she found out I was walking away from my parents' money to join the Army, she dumped me."

"Wow." Sophia slid back down in the bed. "I'm sorry."

"I'm not," Blade said. "I'm glad I learned her true colors before we did something stupid like get married. We would probably have ended up divorced, or worse, bickering like my parents."

Silence stretched between them for a few long moments. Then Sophia offered, "You know not every woman is after money."

"Maybe not, but they want something else that I'm not capable of giving." His tone was hard, unbending.

"And that is?" she asked.

"Stability."

Sophia's heart stuttered but she pressed on. "Stability could mean different things to different people."

"Maybe so, but as a Delta I don't see that happening in my life." The ice in the glass clinked as if he swirled it around. "Not as long as I'm a member of the military."

It was none of her business, but she had to know. "Do you think you'll ever let yourself fall in love again?" Sophia's breath lodged in her throat, awaiting his response.

He didn't answer for a long time. "I'm not sure I know what love is. My parents sure didn't set a good example of it."

"I guess I was lucky," she said. "My parents did. I asked my dad once what it felt like to be in love. How would I know when *I* fell in love? He answered with a question. *How would you feel if that person was no longer with you?* If the answer was broken-hearted, then that's love. That kind of helped me through the death of both my parents at the same time."

"How so?" Blade asked.

"Knowing that they went together meant neither

one suffered a broken heart." Her chest tightened at the memory. "Blade?"

"Yes, Sophia."

"As your friend… I hope you let yourself fall in love again. You deserve to be loved and to be happy." She didn't want him to say anything after that, so she added, "Goodnight, Blade."

"Goodnight, Sophia."

She reflected on her father's words. If Blade were to leave her life, would she be heartbroken? She thought long and hard about it, and the answer was yes. But she also loved him enough that she wanted him to be happy. If it wasn't with her, well, then he would be happy. That's all that mattered.

Just because he'd kissed her once didn't mean that he was in love with her. She'd rather he fell in love with her, but she couldn't make somebody fall in love with her. Either they did or they didn't. She wasn't convinced that he didn't love her. There'd been something in that kiss, and she had the rest of the week to figure it out.

CHAPTER 8

BLADE FINISHED his drink and set his glass on the coffee table. He turned and laid his head on one arm of the couch and draped his legs over the other. At least the cushions were soft.

He lay awake for a long time staring up at the ceiling. Had he ever felt broken-hearted over any woman who'd left his life?

No. Not even the woman he'd thought he was in love with. Her walking out on him hadn't broken his heart. He'd been pretty young then and was probably more in love with the idea of having someone to come home to than actually loving the person.

His thoughts came around to Sophia. She was his friend, and he loved living next door to her. He looked forward to seeing her every time he came home from deployment. When Rucker, Mac and Bull's women had shown up at the airport, Blade had found himself looking around for Sophia's red hair and green eyes. He'd been disappointed, and even more so when she hadn't come to his house when he'd finally made it home that night.

If Calderón had gotten away with Sophia before Blade had had a chance to rescue her, would he have been broken-hearted? That all out desperate feeling when he had seen those men dragging her away, would he have felt the same way if it had been anybody else that he was responsible for? Maybe, but even more so because it was Sophia. With his ears straining for every little sound, he drifted off to sleep.

The wind picked up during the night, tossing the palm trees outside the bungalow. The slapping sound the fronds made woke him.

Something else caught his attention. Was it a whimper coming to him from the bedroom? Blade rose from the couch, stretched and worked the kinks out of his neck as he hurried toward the bedroom.

Sophia laid tangled in the sheets, her arms and legs thrashing. "No," she moaned.

Blade stopped by the side of her bed and touched her shoulder. "Sophia, you're having a bad dream. Wake up."

She moaned again, her eyes remaining shut.

He leaned over her. "Sophia, sweetheart, wake up."

Sophia jerked awake, her eyes opening wide.

When she spotted him, she cried, "Blade." She flung her arms around his neck and clung to him.

He lifted her in his arms and sat on the bed cocooning her body with his. He smoothed his hand over her curls and spoke to her in a soothing tone. "It'll be okay. Those bad guys aren't here. I'm here. I'll take care of you."

She buried her face in his neck, her body trembling.

He crooned to her, speaking in hushed tones until her trembling subsided.

Her hands slid over his chest, and she pressed closer, draping one of her legs over his.

"Sophia?" Blade whispered into her ear. "Are you awake?"

She murmured. "Mmm."

"No more bad dreams?"

She shook her head, her soft curls brushing against his skin, stirring him.

He drew in a shaky breath and let it out. "I should go back to the living room."

Her arm tightened around his chest "No. Please stay."

Blade was afraid that if he stayed, he wouldn't be able to resist exploring each freckle on her skin.

Her hand slipped from his chest down to his torso.

Blade's groin tightened. If he didn't move immediately, he'd do something he might regret.

When her hand reached the elastic of his boxer shorts, he felt a moan rising up his throat. Now. He had to move now.

Her hand slipped beneath the elastic of his boxer shorts and skimmed across his engorged shaft.

His breath lodged in his throat.

Oh, sweet Jesus. It was too late. He tipped her chin up and stared down into her pretty green eyes reflecting the light from the bathroom. "Do you know what you're doing to me?"

She chuckled as her warm fingers circled him. "I have a good idea."

He swept a strand of her hair back behind her ear. "You know this could ruin a perfectly good friendship?"

Sophia's forehead wrinkled. "Screw friendship. Look, I want this. No strings attached. No expectations. Just stay with me tonight. Then, you can date all the women in the world, and I won't say a thing. I'll just be another notch on your bedpost." She gave him a stiff smile. "And I'm okay with that."

"But what if I'm not okay with it? Sophia, you deserve better than that. You're my friend, and I value that friendship."

Her hand tightened on his erection and slid up and back down where she fondled his balls.

A groan escaped his mouth. "This isn't right."

"Does it feel right?" she asked. "It feels right to me." Her hand tightened.

"Damn, Sophia." He groaned again. "Yes, it does."

"Then go with it," she whispered.

The walls he'd erected around the feelings he had for her crumbled. He drew in a deep breath and let it out. "Well, if we're going to do this, we're going to do this right."

A smile spread across her face. "I like the way you're thinking."

He flipped her onto her back, leaned over her and captured her mouth in a deep, crushing kiss.

She opened to him and met his tongue with hers.

When he finally broke the kiss, she laughed, gasping for air. "Nice start, soldier. What else ya got?"

"Sassy much?" He shook his head and bent to press a kiss to the side of her neck just below her ear.

She leaned her head back, giving him more access to her long slender throat.

Blade kissed a path down her neck, stopping to press a kiss to the pulse beating at the base of her throat. He skimmed over her collarbone and downward, pressing his lips against the soft jersey material of her T-shirt and capturing one of her breasts in his mouth.

Sophia arched her back, grabbed the hem of her T-shirt, pulled it up over her head and tossed it to the floor, giving him full access to her skin.

He accepted her offering, drawing her nipple into his mouth and sucking gently. Then he flicked it with his tongue and rolled the hard little bead between his teeth.

Sophia writhed and moaned beneath him.

His blood pushed molten heat throughout his body, and he grew harder with each passing second. From that breast, he moved to the other one and gave it the same attention. Then he moved down her torso one rib at a time. When he reached the edge of her shorts, he paused. He might be ruining a friendship, but he wouldn't ruin her life. He climbed out of the bed and went into the other room to where he'd left his duffle bag. Once he'd found his shaving kit and the protection he'd stashed there, he was back in a flash.

Sophia smiled. "I thought maybe you'd changed your mind."

He held up the packet. "No, I didn't change my mind, but I didn't lose it either."

She nodded.

His brow furrowed. "I haven't changed my mind, have you?"

She swung her legs over the side of the bed and held out her hand for the packet.

His lips curled up on the corners as he handed over the condom. "What are you doing?"

She gave him a slow sexy smile. "Taking matters into my own hands." She stared up at him, locking her gaze with his, and then she slipped her hands beneath the elastic of his boxer shorts and pushed them down his hips, letting them fall to the floor.

He stepped free of them.

She reached for his hardened shaft and ran both hands over the length of it, pausing to fondle him at the base.

His breath caught and held, arrested in his lungs. For him, there was no going back. He was coming apart at the seams and damned himself all the way to hell for what he was about to do to her after she did whatever it was she was going to do him.

Sophia leaned forward and touched her tongue to the tip of his erection.

His cock jerked automatically. Blade groaned.

She looked up. "That hurt? Or was it good?"

He drew in a deep breath to steady his beating heart. "Good," he bit out between clenched teeth. Just being near her mouth made him want to blow.

When she leaned forward again, she took him into her mouth. Her hands gripped his buttocks and pulled him forward until the tip of his cock bumped against the back of her throat. Her mouth was so warm and wet, like he imagined her channel would be.

Sophia's tongue swirled around his shaft as she pushed him back, just enough. Setting the rhythm, she guided him in and out of her mouth, increasing the speed each time.

Blade buried his hands in her hair, loving how the

curls wrapped around his fingers and how she responded to his slightest pressure. Soon, they were moving in sync, the pace growing faster and faster.

When he teetered on the edge of his control, he pulled free of her mouth. He wanted to be inside her when he came.

Sophia smiled up at him, feeling powerful after the control she'd had over him for the few short minutes they'd been together. There was no doubt that he liked what she was doing.

"Your turn," he said, as he settled between her legs with the tip of his shaft touching her entrance. "I want you," he said. "But we're not finished."

She gave him a lazy, sexy smile. "What's keeping you?"

"This," he said, and he worked his way down her body quickly, grabbing hold of her shorts and panties and dragging them down her legs to her ankles and off. Then he kissed a path up the insides of her legs to the center of her desire.

Sophia sucked in a breath and held it. He parted her folds and tapped his tongue to that plump strip of flesh, packed with thousands of nerve endings. When he touched her there, it was as if every one of them ignited.

She gasped and clutched his shoulders.

He flicked her again, and fire burned through her

veins. Her fingernails curled into his skin, and she lifted her hips off the mattress, rising to meet that incredible tongue, wanting more. Every touch pushed her closer to the edge until she vaulted into the stratosphere. Tingling started at her core and spread outward to the very tips of her fingers and toes. She rode wave after wave of sensations until she collapsed against the mattress. Climaxing with Blade should have been enough. But Sophia still wanted more. She wanted to feel him inside her, filling her.

Blade rose up over her and captured her mouth in a deep kiss at the same time as he pressed his shaft to her entrance.

Sophia clutched his bare buttocks in her hands and pressed him in, taking his full length into her slick center.

He paused, giving her time to accommodate his girth. Then he drew out and pushed back in, settling into a slow, steady pace.

Once again Sophia's body tensed at all the sensations running through it. "Faster," she said. Her hands on his ass guided him into the rhythm she preferred.

He obliged, going faster and faster, until he suddenly pulled out and said, "Wait."

Sophia's breath hitched.

"Wait. I almost forgot." He fished in the sheets for the packet that had been left beside them, tore it open with his teeth, and rolled it down over his cock. Then he was back again, pumping in and out of her.

She rose with her hips meeting his, thrust for thrust.

His body tensed beneath her fingertips. He sank into her and held steady, his cock throbbing as he released inside her channel.

For a long moment, she lay there enjoying the feel of him inside of her and wondering how one time would be enough.

Blade dropped down on his elbows and bent to kiss her. Then he rolled, bringing them both to their sides, without losing connection. They lay for a long time together in the most intimate way.

As she lay in his arms Sophia could hear the soft sound of rain on the roof.

Blade smoothed a strand of her hair back behind her ear. "Go to sleep, Sophia."

She snuggled into the crook of his arm and closed her eyes, smiling. She was where she had always wanted to be. She'd enjoy it while it lasted though she was sure it wouldn't be for very long.

CHAPTER 9

WHEN SOPHIA OPENED her eyes again, the pillow beside her was empty, and sun shone through an open window. Sophia stretched, feeling deliciously sore in all the right places.

Blade strode through the door. "Hey, lazy head, get up. Our excursion leaves in fifteen minutes."

She pulled the sheet up to cover her breasts and sat up straight. "Excursion? What excursion? I thought we couldn't go anywhere."

"I made a last-minute reservation on a trip out to Chichen Itza. If we play our cards right, we can dodge whatever cartel spies are hanging out looking for us, but we have to get moving."

Sophia tossed the sheet aside. "Wouldn't you rather stay here?" she asked with a grin.

His eyes smoldered. "Don't tempt me, woman."

"Tempt you?" she grinned. "Is that all it is?"

"More than you know. So, get up, get dressed and let's go."

She pouted. "I was just getting used to the idea of staying in all day."

"We have ruins to climb and lessons to learn about the Mayan people. Get moving." He clapped his hands twice.

Sophia swung her legs over the side of the bed, stood and pranced past Blade wearing nothing but a smile. "Your loss."

He groaned. "And don't I know it."

She dressed in shorts, running shoes and a tank top. She'd brushed her teeth and pulled her hair up into a messy bun, plunking a hat on top to cover all her hair. She hid her eyes with a pair of sunglasses and looked up at Blade. "Will this do?" she asked.

"Great disguise, but if you've got a lightweight jacket to cover your arms, that would be good too."

"I'll be right back." She ducked into her bedroom and pulled out a light windbreaker and slipped it over her shoulders. When she returned, she found Blade wearing a polo shirt, khaki slacks, hiking boots, a Cancún baseball cap and a pair of sunglasses.

She hated the thought of him hiding his sleek black hair and gorgeous blue eyes, but better to disguise and get out without being detected than having a tail on them all day.

Rather than follow the path up to the hotel, they slipped around behind the bungalows and took a maintenance road leading to the hotel. They arrived just in time to catch the bus that would take them out to Chichen Itza. Blade and Sophia climbed aboard the large bus with other tourists, taking a seat near the rear.

"Did you see our bouncers from last night?" she whispered.

"I thought I saw one standing beside the resort's front door." He nodded toward the man. "I don't think he saw us."

Sophia grinned. "Good. Maybe we'll have a nice day after all."

"I hope so," he said. "I hate to think we might be pushing our luck."

As the bus traveled the road out to Chichen Itza, Sophia and Blade took every opportunity and curve to look behind them to see if they were being followed. As far as they could tell, they weren't.

Eventually, Sophia relaxed against her seat.

Blade reached for her hand and took it in his.

It was looking more and more like a perfect day with the sun softly shining after freshly fallen rain. When they arrived at the ruins, the bus parked alongside several other buses filled with tourists. People climbed out and started the long hike through the jungle to the temple.

Blade maintained his hold on Sophia's hand, much to her pleasure.

Once they reached the base of the temple, Blade smiled at Sophia. “Are you up for a climb?”

She looked up at the steep stairs, shaking inside. “Did I ever tell you I have a fear of heights?”

His brow furrowed. “You don’t have to do it if you don’t want to.”

“Are you going up?” she asked.

He shook his head. “Not without you.”

“Then let’s do it. You might have to lead me back down, because I might have to close my eyes to descend.”

He squeezed her hand. “Seriously, you don’t have to do this if you don’t want to.”

Sophia lifted her chin. “I like to challenge my fears. Most often, it pays off.”

“Then hold on tightly to my hand,” Blade said.

“Oh, you don’t have to tell me twice.” Sophia held his hand in a death grip as they started up the steep steps. By the time she got to the top, she was breathing hard. “I need to work out more.”

Blade wasn’t breathing hard at all. He turned around and looked out at the view. “This is amazing.”

Sophia made it a point to stare straight out. “Yeah, just don’t look down.”

Blade chuckled. “Not yet anyway.”

His words made her look down, and she swayed. “Holy crap.”

His hand came up to steady her. “It’ll be all right.

I'll be right with you and hold your hand all the way down. You just have to take it one step at a time."

As Blade instructed her, Sophia took it one step at a time, only looking at that one step, not all the way down to the bottom.

Though they moved painfully slowly, they arrived safely at the bottom, and they didn't take anybody down in front of them.

Sophia wanted to drop to a prone position on the ground and kiss the dirt, but she restrained herself. Thankfully, they had a long hike back to the bus, which gave her time to stop shaking.

They'd almost made it back to the parking area when Blade stopped her in her tracks, spun her around and kissed her, long and hard.

When he raised his head, Sophia laughed. "What was that for?"

"I needed a reason to stop suddenly, and kissing you was just as good as any other reason."

Sophia snorted. "Wow, I'm underwhelmed. Why'd you need to stop suddenly?"

"Don't look now," he said, "but guayabera man is standing beside our bus."

Sophia swore and turned slowly. Just as Blade had said, the guy who had worn the guayabera shirt the night before at the lounge was talking to the bus driver outside the bus they'd arrived in.

Sophia swore softly. "How are we going get on the bus with him standing there?"

Blade shook his head. "We're not. We're going to get on a different bus."

"Won't they notice that they've got two extra passengers?" she asked.

"We'll sneak aboard, sit way at the back and duck down low."

"What if the bus isn't going to our hotel?"

"I'd almost guarantee it's not, but anything is better than going back with that man following us every step of the way." Blade's gaze remained on the man talking to their bus driver. "We can catch a cab or something else to get back to our hotel."

Sophia nodded, glad they didn't have to run the gauntlet of having to go past guayabera man to get on a bus. If it meant they'd be a little inconvenienced getting back to their hotel, that would be fine. As long as they got back in one piece.

They waited for a large group to board a bus on the far end of the parking lot. Sophia recognized the name of the resort as the one that was next to the resort where they were staying. If anything, they could walk. They blended in with the others and got aboard, aiming for the last seats on the bus.

Fortunately, there was enough room that they didn't displace anybody else, and when the tour guide made his count, they ducked low behind the seats.

The bus pulled out of the parking lot. They looked back at the bus they should have taken. Their tour group had already boarded, and the bus driver was still standing outside, talking to guayabera man and, apparently, looking around for his missing passengers.

Sophia felt bad for the bus driver, but not bad enough to risk their lives.

They made it back to the neighboring resort without incident.

"We can take a cab back or walk along the beach," Blade suggested.

"The beach, please," Sophia said.

They walked through the resort and out onto the sand where they stripped off their shoes and carried them. They walked along, holding hands like any other young couple on vacation, only Sophia knew that Blade was there as a friend and protector. Not as her lover, although last night had been pretty wonderful. But she'd promised him no strings.

Now, she was regretting that promise.

They were able to sneak up behind their bungalow, searching the shadows for any suspicious characters hanging around. The two bouncers from the evening before were nowhere to be seen. They only spotted a lone female stopping to smell the bougainvillea in front of the bungalow next to theirs.

When Blade started to step out toward the front door of their bungalow, Sophia grabbed his arm. "What if that woman is part of the cartel?"

Blade frowned. "Good point."

"You in a hurry?" Sophia asked.

He shook his head. "Not at all. We can wait."

And they did.

The woman took her time smelling the bougainvillea. Then she straightened, glancing right and left before setting out on the path toward the hotel. She stopped halfway up the path and turned, looking at the last bungalow.

"I'd say she looks pretty suspicious, don't you?" Sophia asked.

"Maybe. Unless she's waiting for someone who didn't show up, she has no reason to turn around and look back in our direction," Blade said.

Sophia nodded. "We might put her on our 'to be watched' list."

The woman disappeared around a corner.

"Well, if we can't see her, she can't see us," Blade said. "Let's go in." He entered the bungalow first. "Let me check to make sure it's safe." He spent a few seconds checking the bedroom and bathroom. When he came out, he grinned. "All clear."

Sophia laughed. "Is this what you do at all the hotels you stay at?"

He shook his head. "No, only at the ones where the cartel might be mad at me."

"Or me," Sophia said. "After all, I did hit Calderón in the back of the head with a board."

Blade grinned. "Yes, and I was impressed that you jumped into the fray."

"I wasn't going to let it be three to one. It was bad enough two to one. Although you were doing a good job of it."

He dipped his head. "Thank you. But you're right, I didn't see that other guy coming. What do you want to do for dinner tonight?"

Sophia tilted her head. "We could go to a different resort and have dinner at one of their restaurants, since the cartel knows that we live here for now."

"Sounds like a good plan," Blade said. "I do know of a good seafood restaurant in Cancún that we could go to. But that might be pushing our luck."

Sophia nodded. "One night in downtown Cancún got us into this pickle. Why risk a second shot at it?"

"Agreed," Blade said.

"Although, other than having to take a different bus back, I enjoyed my day," Sophia said. "I consider it a bonus that we got to walk along the beach."

"Me, too." Blade patted his flat stomach. "But now, I'm kind of hungry."

Sophia frowned. "You know you're right. I didn't get breakfast or lunch."

"Me either," Blade said. "Let's aim for an early dinner. You want the shower first, or do you want me to assume the lead?"

Sophia tipped her head toward the bathroom. "You can go first. I need to grab the clothes I want to wear."

Blade snagged his shaving kit and clothes and

headed for the bathroom. As usual, he left the door ajar so he could listen for any sounds.

Sophia thought it was as good an excuse as any for her to slip out of her clothes and join him in the shower.

His head was under the water when she stepped into the shower stall with him. Very quietly she applied soap to her hands and then smoothed them on his body.

He tensed. "What are you doing, Sophia?"

"I didn't feel safe out in the living room by myself."

"You shouldn't feel safe in here either."

"I do. I feel a whole lot safer when I'm with you." She spread the soap suds all over his chest.

She reached into the soap dish and held up a packet. "I found these on the counter."

"In my shaving kit?" he asked an eyebrow cocked.

She shrugged. "Just thinking ahead."

"What am I going to do with you, Sophia?"

"I have a few ideas." She lathered up more soap and ran her hands over his chest, his shoulders and down his arms to his waist. "Getting the drift?"

His cock hardened.

"Never mind," she said, "I can see you've got the idea." She smiled up at him. "Are you in a big hurry to get food?"

Blade growled. "I'm hungry, but now I'm in the mood for something else besides food."

Sophia captured his gaze. "So am I."

BLADE SLIPPED his arms around Sophia and dragged her against him. He kissed her soundly then grabbed the backs of her thighs and lifted her, until she wrapped her legs around him. Then he pressed her back against the cool tile wall. He must have lost his mind. Making love to Sophia could only mean disaster for their friendship. A friendship he wanted more than anything. Still, he couldn't stop himself as he applied the condom and drove into her slick wetness.

She rode him with her head flung back and her hands braced on his shoulders. Her breath came in short, ragged gasps.

As a lover, she was everything Blade could imagine or want. She was also his neighbor and his friend. When they returned from Cancún, what then? They couldn't pick up where they'd left off. Things would be changed. It would be awkward.

He slipped in and out of her. She rested her hands on his shoulders as he rode her hard. She climaxed with him, shouting his name.

When they could breathe again, he soaped her body and washed her hair, and then rinsed her off beneath the shower spray.

She returned the favor, touching every part of his body and making him want even more.

When they stepped out of the shower, they dried each other off, taking longer than necessary by kissing the dry spots as they worked their way over each other's bodies. If they didn't stop touching each other, they'd never make it out of the bungalow.

But it was so hard to stop.

Blade cleared his throat and took a step backward. "So, what do you want for dinner tonight?" Personally, he'd rather stay in and order out, having somebody deliver food to the room. The more time he could spend alone with Sophia, the better. Damn, he was in deep.

He'd already broken his promise to his teammates by sleeping with Sophia. She'd given him carte blanche with no strings attached, which still didn't make it right.

Guilt knotted his belly. He'd known she was a good neighbor and good friend, but he hadn't known how much fun she was to be with, and how sexy and passionate she was in bed. If he wasn't careful, he'd start thinking down the path of wanting to wake up with her every morning for the rest of his life.

Sadly, he wasn't marriage material. Not with his upbringing and his job. Not that Rucker, Dash, Mac and Bull hadn't proven they could find somebody who could love them even in their current jobs. Mac and Dash had it even worse. Their women were on the road as much as they were as a war correspondent and a performer. They had a lot more confidence and optimism in their ability to maintain a long-distance relationship, and their women seemed happy enough to take whatever bits and pieces they could have of them.

His teammates' ladies were all strong and able to take care of themselves in most situations. For that matter, so was Sophia. As a waitress and bartender, she had to defend herself on a daily basis. She might look all soft and feminine, but she was tough and capable.

"Let's order something in," Sophia said. "I don't feel like getting dressed up and putting on makeup."

"Deal," Blade said. "I think I'll have it delivered to our favorite security guy up front and have him bring it to us. One less unfamiliar face."

Sophia smiled. "Good point. Think he'll mind?"

Blade shook his head. "He told me to come to him for anything we might need." He grinned. "We need food."

Blade placed an order for a seafood platter to be delivered to the front desk. He made a call to the security desk and asked for Ramón, the same man who had walked them to their bungalow the night before. He spoke with him in Spanish and arranged to have Ramón bring their food to them when it arrived.

"In the meantime," Sophia stared through the glass of the patio door, "do you think we could sit on our deck and enjoy the remaining light in the sky before it gets dark?"

"That's a possibility. Let me clear it first. And you might want to wear your big floppy hat." Blade opened the sliding glass door and stepped out onto the deck. He made a complete circle around the bungalow, looking for anybody hanging around, and then he walked out onto the beach to check to make sure the suspicious woman was gone, and that none of the bouncers they'd seen the night before had made an appearance.

Most of the beach goers had gone in, with just a couple of families left gathering their belongings and their children. Before long, the beach would be empty except for those brave enough to walk at night in the moonlight. He didn't see anything that would keep them from sitting out on the deck.

When he returned to the bungalow, he found Sophia standing near the sliding glass doors in the shadows. "All clear."

Sophia sighed. "Good. It looks amazing at this time of day with so few people on the sand."

"Would you like a glass of wine?" Blade asked, heading for the kitchenette.

"Yes, please," Sophia said. "I would love a glass."

"Wait here, and we'll go out together." He poured two glasses of wine and carried them out to the porch.

After Sophia took her seat in a lounge chair, Blade

handed her a glass and then he settled in the lounge chair next to her. They had a good view of the beach, but not the sunset. It would set behind them. Still, he enjoyed the sound of the waves and the salty tang in the air. The rain from the night before had evaporated, making the land steamy. They sipped their wine while talking about the Mayan ruins they'd seen that day and other places they'd like to visit in Mexico and South America.

"One of these days, I want to go to Machu Picchu in Peru," Sophia said.

Blade nodded. "That's on my bucket list, too. I've heard wonderful things about it."

"I guess I'll have to save a lot of tip money," she said with a crooked smile. "Or go to work as an accountant and waitress at night."

"If you don't want to be an accountant, why don't you cross train into something else?" Blade asked.

"I really haven't given accounting much of a chance. It reminded me too much of my folks and their passing. I need to give myself permission to move on, but I don't want to leave Sarge high and dry at the Salty Dog. He's been so good to me."

"I'm sure he could find somebody to replace you. And if you don't want to give up working at the bar, you could work part time for him like you said."

She smiled over the rim of her glass. "That's what I was thinking."

Before long, a knock sounded at the door of the bungalow.

Blade rose from his lounge chair. "I think we should take it inside now," he said to Sophia.

She nodded and got up with him. Sophia followed him into the room, and they closed the sliding glass doors.

While Blade answered the main door to the bungalow, Sophia closed the blackout curtains over the patio door.

Before opening the door, Blade checked who it was, and then held the door wide. Ramón, the security guard, carried a box into the bungalow and laid it onto the table.

"Thank you, Ramón," Sophia said.

"*De nada,*" he replied. The security guard spoke to Blade in Spanish explaining that he'd had a couple of men asking questions of the other guards and some of the staff members, wanting to know where the two of them were staying. At first, they'd only had Sophia's first name, but before long, they were asking for them by their full names. Both of them. "And did the staff tell them which bungalow we were in? There was some confusion at the front desk. One of the clerks thought that we were in the hotel proper—and we were supposed to be—until we were upgraded to the bungalow."

"To your benefit, I understand the people in the room you were originally assigned were surprised by a visit from some of those men. Our staff escorted them out, but they will be back. I spoke with management and suggested that we move you to a sister resort."

Blade shook his head, his lips pressing into a thin line. "They would just follow us there."

The security guard nodded. "The manager did change the name on the reservation so that others couldn't look in the system and find you."

"Remind me to thank him," Blade said. "What is the likelihood of a cartel attack on the resort?"

The guard shrugged. "Not very likely. The resorts bring in money and employ a lot of hard-working people. For the most part, they'll wait until you leave the resort. If you choose to take part in one of the excursions, you might want to use the name that the manager set up for you. I believe it is John and Jane Smith."

"We'll do that. Thank you for the information and thank you for bringing our food to us."

The guard nodded. *"De nada."*

When the security guard left, Sophia raised an eyebrow. "That was a long conversation. I really need to brush up on my Spanish."

Blade conveyed the information the security guard had given him.

"So, are we back to being trapped in our bungalow?" Sophia asked. "And now, is our bungalow at risk?"

"I'll see if we can get moved to a different bungalow tomorrow. It might help to switch it up a bit."

Sophia's lips pressed into a thin line. "All because some spoiled little cartel brat got a boo-boo, and Daddy is taking his side."

Blade nodded. "That about sums it up. In the meantime, we have food."

They settled into eating shrimp, crab legs, and crab cakes, polishing it off with a glass of wine.

"We don't have to go anywhere tomorrow. We can stay in," Sophia said.

"I think we'll be all right as long as we use the names that the manager set us up with. Besides, I was looking forward to a little snorkeling."

Sophia grinned. "Does that mean we're going to the Isla Mujeres?"

He nodded. "If I can get us in at the last minute before it fills up."

"Great. I was afraid we were going to miss out on the snorkeling, and I've never been snorkeling in a place like this."

"You're going to love it. It's so clear, and the fish and coral are very colorful."

When they finished eating, they cleaned up and put the remaining food away in the mini refrigerator. They'd have it for breakfast the next morning before they set out on their excursion. Afterward, they settled on the couch together, drinking wine.

Sophia waited to see what Blade would do after all that had happened that day. Would he insist on sleeping on the couch again? When he didn't make a move to go to bed, she stood, took his wine glass from him, set it on the coffee table and held out her hand. "The night isn't over," she said. "I know you have another packet in your shaving kit. I saw it."

"I don't know, Sophia," Blade hedged.

"We've already stepped over that line," she reminded him. "We're going to be here for a few more days. Why not enjoy it?" She took his hand and pulled him to his feet. "Do I have to twist your arm?" She smiled up at him. "Because I know how to do that."

"You don't see me arguing," he said as he followed her into the bedroom.

They stripped their clothes off before they made it to the bed. They made love until midnight, exploring each other's bodies and enjoying lying naked together.

Blade was the last one to close his eyes, his gaze feasting on Sophia with her face flushed and her strawberry-blond eyelashes brushing against her cheeks. She might consider her freckles a nuisance, but Blade loved all of them. He enjoyed discovering where they were on every part of her body.

Blade lay awake thinking about what the security guard had said. Maybe they would be better off staying in the resort hotel with the relative security provided by the staff. They'd done fairly well dodging the cartel on their way to Chichen Itza and back. Going out might be like playing with fire. The longer they played, the bigger chance they had of getting burned.

So far, the men had only asked questions. Nobody had made a move to accost them.

Blade wondered what they were waiting for. Not that he wanted them making a move, but not knowing was getting to him. It was times like these that he really needed to talk to members of his team. He left the bed, went into the living area and dialed Rucker's number.

"Yeah, Blade, what's up?" Rucker answered, his voice groggy.

"Just need a second opinion."

"Hold on, let me go into the living room. I don't want to wake Nora." Less than a minute later Rucker said, "Shoot."

Blade explained what had happened since the incident at the cathedral.

"And nobody's made a move yet?" Rucker asked.

"Not a single move," Blade said. "But they're watching."

"I don't know what to tell you, other than keep Sophia close," Rucker said. "Really close."

"I am," Blade said. Closer than he'd admit to Rucker. The team didn't need to know that he'd already crossed the line with Sophia. They'd give him hell. At that moment, he didn't need their hell, he needed help.

"And just so you know..." Rucker said, "we all decided to stay in the Fort Hood area. Except Dash who went up to Dallas to see Sunny. Even so, I expect him back by tomorrow. So, if you need us, let us know."

Blade sighed. He felt better knowing he could trust his brothers to be there for him. "Thanks, Rucker. It's good to know you guys have my back."

"Always, man."

After he hung up, he felt a little better. Knowing his team was only a phone call and a plane ride away, he went back to bed and laid down next to Sophia.

She snuggled up next to him and rested her head and arm on his chest with one leg sliding over his hips.

He pulled her close and pressed a kiss to her forehead. He liked the way she smelled, like flowers and sunshine. He hoped that he would be enough to keep her safe for the rest of their vacation.

CHAPTER 10

SOPHIA WOKE in Blade's arms the next morning luxuriating in the strength of the muscles surrounding her. He made her feel safe, and she liked that.

"How does coffee and leftover shrimp sound to you?" he asked, his voice rumbling against her ear.

"Actually, that sounds pretty good. Want me to get up and heat it up for you?" she asked.

"I was thinking I'd get it for you."

She tipped her head up to look him in the eye. "How about we do it together?"

Sophia slipped a T-shirt over her head, and Blade pulled on a pair of shorts.

They padded barefooted into the kitchenette where the coffeemaker sat on the counter.

While Blade made coffee, Sophia got the leftovers out of the refrigerator and popped them into the microwave. Soon, they were seated on the outside porch enjoying the sunrise, coffee and shrimp. It was almost as if they were on a regular vacation without any trouble from the cartel.

"I'm looking forward to snorkeling today." Sophia sipped her coffee, careful not to burn her tongue.

"I thought about that all last night," Blade said.

She smiled over the rim of her mug. "Did you come to any conclusions?"

"I almost feel like we shouldn't go. I called Rucker and asked for his advice."

"Oh, yeah?" Her eyebrows rose. "And what did he say?"

"He didn't know what to do either," Blade's lips twisted. "He just said keep you close."

"Well, I'd say you've done a pretty good job of that."

Blade smiled over at her and held out his hand. She took it.

"I hate standing around worrying, and then nothing happens." She set her mug on the table beside her lounger. "Makes you wonder what they're waiting on. Or, if we're just being paranoid."

"I'd thought the same thing," Blade said. "But better safe than sorry."

"If it's all paranoia, then we've wasted an entire vacation."

Blade squeezed her hand. "All right, we'll go snorkeling, but we'll sneak in at the last minute. In fact, I think we'll make reservations with another resort. An independent outfitter."

"You make the arrangements, I'm going to get ready." Sophia left the lounge chair and entered the bungalow.

Blade went online to find a reputable outfitter offering a snorkeling trip to Isla Mujeres. He made the arrangements with only an hour to spare and hurried into the bungalow to let Sophia know where they had to be and when.

Dressed in their disguises, they left the bungalow and walked along the beach to the next resort, where they caught a cab from there.

Blade maintained situational awareness all the while, checking his rear, looking for anybody following them. He felt confident that they'd made a clean getaway.

Once they were on the catamaran and had set sail from the port, he relaxed. Between Cancún and the Isla Mujeres, the catamaran crew found a quiet cove and stopped so that everybody could get off and snorkel in the reefs.

Sophia was amazed at all she saw. Different fish, a turtle and beautiful coral. The best part was that she got to enjoy it with Blade. The day couldn't have been more perfect. They enjoyed sandwiches that the catamaran crew had provided, and Painkiller drinks.

The crew was beginning to gather things for the return trip when a speed boat and a couple of jet skis roared toward them. The jet boat aimed straight for the catamaran.

The captain of the tour boat started the engines and tried to maneuver out of its way.

At the last moment, the jet boat spun sideways throwing a massive wave onto the catamaran. Sophia got caught in the wave and washed overboard, along with a man and his fiancée.

Sophia went under and fought to get to the surface. She'd removed her life vest and had been lying in the sun. Fortunately, she was a strong enough swimmer to get to the surface and grab a gulp of air. Before she could get oriented, a jet ski swept in beside her. The man driving it yanked her up onto the jet ski, draping her over his lap.

She tried pushing against his thigh and against the side of the jet ski, anywhere to get some leverage, but he smacked her face hard enough her head spun. The man driving the jet ski pulled away from the catamaran.

"No!" Sophia cried as the catamaran and the people on it grew smaller in the distance. Waves splashed in her face, choking off her screams.

BLADE HADN'T BEEN able to reach Sophia in time to catch her before she'd been swept overboard. He held onto the deck rail as the wave washed over the boat and its occupants.

Unable to stop what was happening, Blade watched as Sophia was swept off the boat. He prayed she hadn't hit her head on her way over and sunk unconscious below the surface.

When the catamaran rocked back upright, Blade searched the water for any sign of Sophia. At that moment, a jet ski zoomed past them, the rider looking suspiciously like one of the barrel-chested bouncers from the lounge. He circled the side of the boat where people had been dumped into the water.

Three heads popped up out of the water. A man and two women. Blade could easily identify Sophia because of her pale skin and freckled face.

Apparently, the man on the jet ski had as easy a time identifying her as well. He swooped in, grabbed her by her arm and yanked her onto the jet ski.

His heart in his throat, Blade dove in as close as he could get to the jet ski.

By the time he surfaced, the jet ski was pulling away from the catamaran with Sophia draped across the man's lap.

The jet boat and jet skis sped away.

Blake could do nothing about it. He swam to the catamaran, pulled himself out of the water and hurried to the boat captain.

"You have to follow them," he demanded.

The captain shook his head. "I can't. I have two people in the water. I have to get them out first. There's no way we can catch up."

"Then you have to get me back to Cancún. I have to report this as soon as possible." Blade's gaze followed the boat and jet skis as they disappeared into the distance. His chest was tight, and his gut knotted.

"Once we get the people aboard, I have to get a headcount. Then we can leave."

Blade pushed past the captain and hurried to the end of the boat where he and the crew helped the other woman out of the water and then the man.

The captain performed a headcount of the passengers and crew. Blade did his own. Their counts matched. They had the same number of passengers as when they'd left the marina at Cancún, minus one.

Sophia.

Blade paced the deck all the way back to Cancún. As soon as the boat pulled up to the dock, he jumped off, pulled his cellphone out of the waterproof bag he'd carried aboard and hit the number for Rucker.

"You must be missing us badly," Rucker answered.

"The cartel got Sophia."

"Shit," Rucker said. "I'll mobilize the team. As soon as I know our ETA, I'll let you know."

"Thanks," Blade said. "Out here."

Blade didn't know how or when they'd get to Cancún, but his team would be there for him and Sophia as soon as they could get a flight to Mexico. In the meantime, he had to gather all the intel he could.

He suspected the cartel wasn't done. By kidnapping Sophia, they could lure him out into the open so they could capture him, too. Then they could exact their revenge on him for what he'd done to Calderón and his men.

As far as Blade was concerned, the sooner they found him the better. At least then he'd know where they'd taken Sophia. Then he could come up with a plan to free them both.

Not having a whole lot of faith in his ability to find Sophia and bring her back, Blade caught a cab back to the resort and immediately went in search of the housekeeper, Maria. He also wanted to talk to Ramón. Unfortunately, his favorite security guard was not yet on duty.

He had to find Maria. Maybe she knew someone who could help.

Blade started with the concierge, asking where he might find the housekeeper, Maria.

The concierge referred him to Hector, the housekeeping staff director. He could find the director in the laundry room. After getting directions, Blade hurried there, desperate to find Maria as soon as possible.

Hector turned out to be a short barrel of a man. He carried an electronic tablet and stood with a couple of women who were folding sheets.

Blade hurried up to Hector and spoke to him in Spanish telling him what he needed. He asked where he could find Maria, the housekeeper who cleaned the last bungalow by the beach.

Hector glanced down at the tablet with a frown, touched the screen several times and finally glanced up to tell Blade that Maria should be cleaning the bungalows. That was her primary responsibility. Hector checked his tablet again and stated that Blade should find her in the bungalow past number fifteen. That was the last one she had completed and marked off. The man tilted his head and narrowed his eyes. "Is there a problem?" he asked in English.

Was there a problem? Blade almost laughed. Hell yes, there was a problem. Sophia had been taken and he had to find her as soon as possible. "I wanted to ask her for extra towels," Blade stated.

"I can have Maria bring you the towels. No need to tell her yourself. If you need anything, all you have to do is ask the concierge for it. My staff will see to you." Hector pulled his radio off the clip on his belt and spoke into the microphone.

"Thank you." Blade left the laundry room and raced back out to the long sidewalk in front of the bungalows, counting off as he passed one after the other. He reached number fifteen and didn't slow until he spotted the cleaning cart outside of bungalow number seventeen, a couple doors down from the very last bungalow. Maria stepped out, carrying an armload of linens.

He called out, "Maria."

Startled, the housekeeper glanced up. "*Señor* Blade."

In Spanish, he explained the situation of how Sophia had been abducted from their catamaran excursion.

Maria wrung her hands, a frown pulling her brow low on her forehead. "*No Bueno. No bueno.*"

"I notified the Mexican police, but they were no help," he told her.

Maria snorted. "They work for the cartel."

Blade raked a hand through his hair, his heart pounding in his chest. "If you know anybody who might have a connection to the cartel, and know where they might have taken Sophia, I need that person's name. I need help."

Maria shook her head. "It is not safe for me to name names."

"If not a name, a location. Anything. I've got to know where they've taken her."

Maria touched his arm. "I'll ask my cousin. He might know someone who can help. They will not be satisfied with just her. They will come after you next." Maria's mouth formed a thin line. "They will exact revenge."

Blade had figured as much. "That's why I need to find Sophia before they find me."

She nodded. "Give me some time. I will contact my cousin."

"We don't have much of time," Blade said.

Maria nodded and pulled a cellphone out of her apron pocket. She walked away, scrolling through her contacts. When she found the one she wanted, she initiated the connection and spoke quietly in Spanish to the person on the other end of the line.

Blade strained to hear and translate her words.

Maria spoke in a soft murmur.

Blade only caught every sixth word or so. From what he did glean from her conversation, she was telling her cousin about Sophia being kidnapped and that the cartel had her.

After a few minutes of rapid-fire Spanish, she ended the call and turned toward him. "My cousin will meet with you at the Iguana Café at four o'clock this afternoon."

"How will I know how to find him?" Blade asked.

Maria shook her head. "Don't worry, he will find you."

With no one else to turn to, Blade nodded. At that moment Maria and her cousin were his only hope. "I'll be there."

Again, Maria touched his arm. "I'm sorry about your woman."

Blade didn't even have the stomach to tell Maria that Sophia wasn't his woman, especially when he was wishing she was.

With a couple of hours to blow before four o'clock he went to the business center of the resort, logged onto the computer and searched for anything and everything he could find on the cartel for that region. He focused on Calderón, the current cartel leader. Searching for his place of residence. He wondered how every social media site could keep track of every person on earth, and yet he couldn't find anything on Calderón's location on the internet. What he needed was a good hacker, or someone associated with the dark web to find Calderón and his location. With his gut knotted and his frustration levels at an all-time high Blade continued to slog through the internet praying for any kind of hope to find Sophia.

As he was sitting at the computer terminal the door opened, and Ramón, the night security guard stepped in. "Ramón, *cómo estás*?

Ramón responded in English. "I am well, but I understand your woman has been taken."

Blade nodded. "Word travels fast. How did you find out?"

"Maria and I share the same cousin and none of us like the cartel. Especially when they attack our loved ones. Too often we pay our dues just to keep them from targeting us, but the resorts are our livelihoods. When the cartels interfere with the guests who bring money to the resort's we are not happy."

"Are you here to tell me anything different than what your cousin's supposed to tell me at four?" Blade asked.

Ramón shook his head. "No, *señor*. I am here to take you to my cousin by four o'clock."

"Don't you have to work tonight?"

Ramón shook his head. "No. This is my night off. I will help you find your woman."

Blade heaved a sigh. "Thank you."

"Targeting tourists is not something we will tolerate. If word gets out that it's not safe at the resorts, people will stop coming. We will lose our jobs and won't be able to put food on the table for our families."

Blade frowned. "Will helping me put you in danger?"

Ramón nodded. "But if someone doesn't stand up to the cartel, then we all fail."

"I don't want to put you in danger," Blade said.

"It is not unusual for resort staff to supplement their income with side jobs like chauffeuring tourists around the Yucatan Peninsula. I will be your chauffeur today."

Blade grinned. "Thank you, and I'll pay you."

"That is not necessary," Ramón said.

"Maybe not, but in keeping with the front of being my chauffeur, it would make it more plausible."

Ramón nodded. "Are you ready?"

Blade pushed to his feet. "Might as well. I wasn't finding much on the internet having to deal with where the cartel stays."

"And you won't find anything there," Ramón said,

"They move often enough to keep other gangs or cartels from targeting them. Hopefully, my cousin will know their latest location."

"And what about your cousin?" Blade asked, "Are we putting him in danger?"

Ramón's lips pressed into a tight line. "My cousin won't care. He hates the cartel."

"Did they do something to make him mad?" Blade asked.

The guard's jaw hardened, and he nodded. "They killed his family. As far as he's concerned, they have nothing to hold over him anymore. He'd like to see them rot in hell."

"Then that makes two of us."

Ramón shook his head. "Make that three." He gave a tight smile. "And if Maria was anybody to be counted, that would be four. There are many more who feel the same, who'd like the cartel to be ended. But as soon as you end one, another gang takes over. Sometimes, it is better to have the enemy you know, than the one you do not."

"True." Blade glanced at his watch. They had half an hour to get to the location he was supposed to meet Maria's cousin. Having Ramón with him would make it easier to determine who the cousin was. And as soon as Ramón dropped him off he could send him on his way so that he wouldn't be involved in case the cartel was there ready to gun him down.

Ramón led the way through the resort hotel

traversing all the back corridors to an exit leading out onto a parking lot near the rear of one of the buildings. Apparently, the parking lot was for employees only, with a mish mash of vehicles parked there. Ramón led him to a dark, four door sedan and opened the back door for him.

"I can ride up front," Blade said.

Ramón shook his head. "Not if I'm chauffeuring you. It is safer for you and for me if the cartel thinks I am only transporting you like an Uber driver."

"Good point," Blade said.

Ramón drove Blade through the less touristy streets of Cancún, stopping at a café where locals enjoyed a meal.

"Our cousin will find you here," Ramón said. "I will wait for you two blocks ahead at the autobody shop. Look for me behind the building. And watch your back."

"How will I know who your cousin is?" Blade asked.

"Don't worry," Ramón said, "He will find you."

Blade climbed out of the car wishing he had a gun or any other kind of protection. The patrons of the café looked up as he stepped in between the occupied tables to find one that was empty.

Without looking too obvious he studied the people at each of the tables. Other than a brief glance in his direction, they returned to their meals, none of them making eye contact with him.

Blade chose an unoccupied table near the rear of the dingy café and sat with his back to the wall. He'd selected the table because there was another empty table beside it and he hoped that Maria and Ramón's cousin would take that seat or sit with him. If Maria's cousin didn't want to be too obvious, he'd take the table beside him.

Blade checked his watch. Four o'clock on the nose. He looked around, hoping to find his contact.

A waiter stopped at his table and dropped a laminated menu in front of him. *"¿Qué quieres beber?"* What do you want to drink?

The thought of eating or drinking anything made Blade's stomach knot even more. He couldn't consider enjoying a meal when Sophia was somewhere possibly being tortured. He glanced at the menu to appear normal in a very abnormal situation. *"Una cerveza."*

The waiter nodded. "*Si, Señor* Blade."

Blade's head shot up and he met the waiter's gaze. How had he known his name?

CHAPTER 11

IN SPANISH, the waiter said, "You may want to check both sides of the menu."

Blade's pulse quickened. He carefully turned the menu over so that only he could see the other side. A folded note was taped to the back. He pulled the note off the back of the laminated menu and pocketed it. He glanced at the waiter and nodded. "Fajita taco, por favor."

The waiter disappeared and returned in a minute with a fajita taco on a plate.

With the note burning a hole in his pocket, Blade waited for a chance to open it while no one was watching.

As the waiter set the plate on the table, two men entered the restaurant. Both had broad-shoulders and dark, heavy eyebrows. They scanned the crowd of guests with narrowed eyes.

Blade's waiter glanced toward them and frowned. He turned to Blade and said in English, "Time to leave." His tone was low and urgent.

As Blade stood, the two men who'd entered the restaurant spotted him and started across the room in his direction. Blade tossed money on the table, grabbed the taco and headed for the back door.

A shout sounded from behind him. As he reached the back exit, he glanced over his shoulder to see the men racing toward him. As they passed the waiter, the one in front tripped and fell on his face. The other one tumbled over the first, landing with a crash on the floor.

The waiter motioned for Blade to continue, then he bent to the jumble of men lying on the floor, apologizing for his clumsiness.

Blade ran out the back door. He headed in the direction of the auto body shop where Ramón had said he'd be waiting. A door slammed open behind him. He glanced over his shoulder to see the two men who had fallen in the café racing after him.

Blade ducked down a side street, dropped on his belly, and rolled beneath what appeared to be an abandoned vehicle.

Footsteps pounded from around the corner onto the side street where Blade hid. He could see the feet of the pursuers as they ran past the vehicle he hid beneath. Once the two men had turned onto the next street, Blade rolled out from beneath the vehicle, and ran back the opposite direction to the alley behind the buildings.

Eventually, he came to a lot filled with vehicles in various stages of repair. Working his way through the numerous vehicles, he found Ramón's dark sedan parked beneath a shade tree.

Blade eased up to the car. After ascertaining it was Ramón behind the steering wheel, Blade slipped into the back seat.

Without a word, Ramón started the engine and drove out of the lot. As they pulled out onto the street, Blade caught a glimpse of the two men who had been chasing him. They turned toward Ramón's vehicle.

Blade ducked down.

Ramón drove past them, heading in the opposite direction from the resorts.

Lying on the back seat, Blade pulled the note out of his pocket and unfolded it, revealing a set of numbers.

"What did our cousin have to tell you?"

Blade frowned and sat up, checking through the rear window for anyone following them. "It appears to be a set of coordinates."

He entered the numbers on his cellphone's map application, but it didn't bring up the location. He tried again. It wasn't working.

"Where to?" Ramón asked.

"I need access to a computer," Blade said.

As Ramón drove, Blade pulled out his cellphone and dialed Rucker's number. It rang and rang and rang, until finally his voicemail came on.

"Leave a message, I'll get back with you," his voice said.

"Call me," Blade said and ended the call. Where the hell was Rucker? He tried Mac's number and got the same response. One by one he went through the members of each member of his team. None of them were answering their cellphones.

The vehicle pulled to a stop and Ramón leaned over the seat.

Blade looked up from his cellphone.

The security guard had stopped in front of an internet café in one of the touristy sections of Cancún.

"I will wait for you here," Ramón said.

Blade got out of the vehicle and hurried into the internet café. Most people had brought their own devices and were using the internet the café provided. There were several computer terminals that could be used as well. He paid the clerk at the counter and sat at one of the empty seats in front of a monitor and keyboard.

He entered the numbers from the note into the search bar and waited to see what came up. When that didn't work, he went to a site that specialized in GPS coordinates and entered the numbers in there. A map appeared on the screen. He switched to a satellite image of the map and zoomed in on the coordinates. It appeared to be nothing more than a spot in the jungle west of Cancún.

Blade switched back to the street map. Several different roads would get him almost all the way there. He studied the location on the big screen of the computer and then entered the coordinates on his cellphone in the same application.

If the coordinates were the location where they'd taken Sophia, he'd need wheels to get there and his team's help to extract Sophia from the cartel's clutches. Where the hell were they?

Once he had the coordinates locked in on the map on his phone, he left the internet café and climbed back into the vehicle where Ramón waited. So, he had coordinates. Did he trust Maria's cousin not to lead him into a trap? "Ramón, what can you tell me about your cousin?"

Ramón pulled out into the road shaking his head. "He and I played soccer together as kids. We both joined the Mexican Army when we were old enough. I stayed four years and got out. I'm not sure what he did. He left the Mexican army, but where he went from there not many people know. Some speculate that he joined the French Foreign Legion."

Which would explain his use of the coordinates, Blade thought. "Why did you leave the Mexican military?" Blade asked.

"Probably the same reason why Maria's cousin

did. We were fighting a losing war within our own country. The cartels rule."

Blade leaned over the back of the seat and showed Ramón the map on his phone. "Based on what Maria's cousin gave me, I assume these are the coordinates where they might have taken Sophia. Are you familiar with these roads?"

Ramón pulled over to the side of the street and shifted into park. He stared at the phone, zoomed in on the roads and nodded. "I am familiar."

"I need to get there."

"If it is a cartel location, they will have guards on the roads coming into the compound."

Blade nodded.

"I would take you there in this vehicle, but you have already been seen in this car."

"And I don't want to draw any more attention than I have to you," Blade said, "I'd prefer to go in alone, but I need transportation."

Ramón shook his head. "You do not have to go in alone. I will go with you, but we need different transportation." He smiled. "And I have a cousin who can help us with that. I will take you there."

Blade sat back in his seat as Ramón zig-zagged through the streets of Cancún, heading south.

Ramón drove up to a stucco walled residence and honked his horn. A minute later a short stocky man opened the gate and allowed Ramón to drive through. Once inside the walled compound Ramón parked the car and got out. He opened the back door for Blade and Blade got out as well.

The yard around the residence was littered with a number of motorcycles and motorcycle parts. The short stocky man who'd opened the gate had grease on his hands and beneath his fingernails. He pulled Ramón into a hug and clapped his hands on his back.

Ramón smiled and laughed and then turned toward Blade. He spoke to his cousin in Spanish.

Their conversation flowed so fast, Blade didn't have a chance to keep up. He only caught a few of the words, not enough to make sense of it.

The short stocky man smiled, nodded and waved a hand around the cluster of motorcycles.

Ramón shook hands with his cousin and then turned to Blade. "Xavier has agreed to loan us two motorcycles."

His cousin left them in the yard, went into the house and came back out with a couple of helmets, handing them over. Then he led them to the two motorcycles that stood apart from the others.

Ramón frowned at Blade. "You have ridden a motorcycle, have you not?"

Blade nodded. "Yes, I have."

Ramón's frown turned into a smile. "Good. We should get going. It's going to be dark soon."

Xavier held up a finger, turned and ran back into the house. He came back out carrying two pistols and a couple of shoulder holsters. He handed them over to Ramón.

Ramón thanked him. "Gracias." He handed one of the shoulder holsters to Blade and waited while he slipped into it and then handed him a forty-five caliber pistol.

Blade dropped the magazine out of the handle, checked that it had bullets and shoved it back into the handle. He turned to Ramón's cousin and nodded. "Gracias."

Xavier went back into the house and came back out with a couple of lightweight jackets for them to put over their shoulder holsters. Complete with their guns and helmets, the two men mounted their motorcycles and drove out of the walled compound.

Ramón led the way through the roads out into the western side of Cancún following highways and then dirt roads.

Blade checked his cellphone map every once in a while, to make sure they were on course. Ramón had a good handle on their direction and led them the right way. For all he knew Ramón could be working with the cartel to capture him as well. But Blade's gut told him that he was one of the good guys.

Ramón slowed and pulled out his own cellphone. He came to a halt on the dirt road and waited for Blade to catch up.

Blade pulled in beside Ramón.

Together, they studied the map where the GPS

coordinates had led them. At some point the roads were no longer displayed on the map and the coordinates were out in the green space. There had to be a road or a track or something to get back to where the coordinates indicated.

"The road has to be here somewhere," Ramón said.

Blade nodded. "We'll go slow until we find it. I'll take the lead from here."

Ramón fell in behind Blade as he drove his motorcycle along the dirt road. After a couple miles passed by and still no sign of a road Blade began to worry that they were on the wrong path. Then he noticed muddy tracks up ahead. He raised his hand and slowed, pulling off to the side of the dirt road and in amongst the bushes where he hid his motorcycle.

Ramón rolled to a stop behind him. They dismounted and left the motorcycles hidden in the trees and underbrush. Moving quietly through the jungle, they paralleled the road up to the point where the muddy tracks lead into the jungle. A perfect hideout for a cartel.

This had to be the place.

Sophia struggled to free herself from the man who had pulled her across the jet ski, but every time she tried to break free, she was hit in the face by a wave and struggled just to breathe. The big jet boat pulled up beside them. The jet ski came to a stop.

With the waves lessened, Sophia was able to break free of the man holding her, and she dropped into the water. When she surfaced, there were men leaning over the boat to grab her arms and yank her out of the water. She fought, kicking and screaming, but she was tired, breathless and too far away from the people on the catamaran. In fact, she could no longer see them. Her heart sank to her knees. She couldn't give up, no matter the overwhelming odds against her. She lifted her chin. "I'm an American citizen. You can't treat me like this."

The men spoke to each other in Spanish and laughed.

"You better let me go or the U.S. military will come down on you."

They spoke to each other again in Spanish and laughed. Then one of them turned to her and said, "The U.S. military can do nothing here. In case you didn't notice you are in Mexico."

At least she knew that one of them could speak English, and quite well at that. "You won't get away with this," she said. "You might as well let me go now. The U.S. government—"

"The U.S. government what?" The man who spoke English snarled at her. "They won't do anything. We get away with murder. They do nothing." He nodded to the other guard.

The other man pulled a roll of duct tape out from under a seat, tore off a small piece and slapped it over her mouth.

Sophia immediately regretted her outburst. Especially when they wrapped duct tape around her wrists and forced her to sit on the back seat of the jet boat. She considered throwing herself over the side of the boat as it took off, but with her wrists bound and her mouth taped shut, she'd struggle to keep her head above water and air in her lungs. She'd have to plan her escape for when they were on dry land.

The jet boat sped along the coast for some time, pulling into a small cove with a pier jutting out. It appeared to be a private pier with no tourists gathering around to witness the men carrying the woman off the jet boat and toss her in a van. The pier and the beach around it appeared deserted. There were no tourists and no witnesses that she could shout to even if she could shout for help.

When Sophia landed on the floor of the van, she slipped out the door onto the ground outside. She hit the dirt, rolled away from the van, pushed to her knees and staggered to her feet. She made it all of five steps before she was grabbed from behind by her hair and yanked to a stop. Sophia wasn't sure where she would have gone, but anywhere was better than the back of the van because she had no idea where they were going to take her next.

The two men lifted her, carried her back to the van and threw her onto the floor.

Her head hit the metal floor so hard she blacked out. When she came to a few moments later, the vehicle was moving along a bumpy, curvy road. They were on paved roads for a while. The van turned off the pavement and rumbled over what had to be gravel. Without a window to look out, she had no idea where they were taking her. Soon even the gravel turned into what felt like a rutted path. Their pace slowed.

What little light had been coming through the front windows dimmed. Sophia couldn't tell if it was because of nighttime or because they were in dense foliage. Either way it was getting dark inside the van.

She pushed to a sitting position. With her arms bound behind her she felt the inside of the van for any kind of rough surface she could grind the tape against to tear it free. She found a rough piece of metal and started sawing at her hands behind her back, trying to get the tape free. Sophia did her best to hide her efforts behind her from the men sitting across from her.

Because her mouth was covered in tape, she couldn't talk to them. And that was just as well. They kept up a running conversation between each other, of which she could only translate a word here and there.

When she got out of this situation, she hoped to

take Spanish so she would never be so clueless as to what others were talking about. She wished that Blade was with her to translate, but then again, if he was with her, he would have gotten her out of this spot already.

Sophia wouldn't accept that she was helpless. She was a strong woman capable of taking care of herself. Well, it was time she proved it.

First things first. She had to get her wrists unbound. Then the next time they stopped, she'd do a better job of making a break for it. Once she was free, she would find her way back to the resort.

By now, Blade would be frantic. No, not frantic. The man would be determined. He'd come up with a plan and find her no matter what. In the meantime, she had to keep herself safe and get herself out of the pickle she found herself in. She didn't want Blade to wade into this quagmire of a cartel and get himself killed.

The van finally stopped, and the door slid open. Based on the shadows, evening had settled in. Gone were the beaches and sand of the coastline. They had brought her deep into the jungle. She had only managed to tear the tape a little bit, but not enough to free her wrists completely. She needed more time with the rough metal inside the van. Still, as soon as they pulled her out of the van, they let go of her long enough that she headbutted the man who spoke English hitting him square in the gut.

He flew backward, landing hard on his ass. The other man hadn't quite been looking when she'd knocked the English-speaking guy to the ground, giving her just the break she needed to make a run for it.

She took off and headed for the trees, figuring that whatever was out there wasn't nearly as bad as the people who'd captured her. She didn't get far before the two men caught up with her, grabbed her and spun her around. The one she'd headbutted smacked her hard in the face busting her lip and making her ears ring. The one who didn't speak English flung her over his shoulder in a fireman's carry, clamping his arms around her legs to keep her from kicking him in the face.

He carried her away from the edge of the forest through a gate into a walled compound, inside which were two main buildings. One was a long narrow structure that could have been barracks for the cartel's minions. The other was more a palatial residence with few windows. She could hear the hum of a generator. The van's headlights lit their way forward into the compound. Other than that, it was pretty dark inside the wall and in the jungle. With the overgrowth of trees, she imagined it would be hard to spot the buildings from a satellite.

The cartel had the perfect location for a stronghold and a hard one to find even for the Delta Force. Her heart sank. She couldn't be guaranteed that

Blade would find her. And even if he did, how would he get inside? Sophia counted two guards at the gate carrying AK-47s.

Blade was but one man. How would he get in here to rescue her, even if he found her?

Her jaw firmed. She would have to find a way out and then find her way back to the resort. It would be easier for her to get out than for him to get in by himself, even though Delta's were known to be very resourceful. Sophia didn't want Blade to risk his life for her. Especially since she was the one who got them in this situation by flirting with Andrés Calderón. As if the mere thought of his name conjured the man, she heard a voice say.

"Ah, so we meet again, *Senorita* Phillips."

The man carrying her dumped her on the ground in front of Calderón. The man's nose was swollen, and his eyes were blackened. His lip curled in a nasty snarl.

Andrés reached down, grabbed the tape across her face, and yanked it off.

It hurt. Sophia fought to keep from showing her pain. At least now she could talk freely. "What's the matter, Andrés?" she asked. "Not as tough as you thought you were? One man took down three of you. I bet your daddy wasn't pleased."

His eyes narrowed. "You think this is all about revenge?"

"Isn't it?" she cocked an eyebrow.

He laughed, reached out, and twirled a finger around one of the strands of her coppery hair. "This is all about supply and demand," he said. "Basic economics. There's demand on the market for redheads. And because there are so few in the supply chain, that makes you in high demand."

When she tried to move her head away to get the strand of hair away from his fingers, he twisted his hand and tugged hard on the strand of hair. "I don't like to disappoint my buyers, especially when they pay good money. And yes, I will use you as bait to get your boyfriend to come looking for you. And when he does, I will exact my revenge."

"So, you're going to let him know where you've kept me?"

Andrés shook his head. "I'm a fool to have let him best me the first time, but no, I'm not that much of a fool."

"And your father is okay with what happened? I'm sure he had words with you. Was he not embarrassed that his only son couldn't handle one man, even when he had three people to help fight against him?"

Andrés's eyes narrowed to a squint. "My father does not own me."

"Oh, and he doesn't clean up your messes?" Sophia raised both eyebrows. "I would think that would make you a liability to him. Does he know that you are trafficking humans?"

Andrés laughed out loud. "Not only does he

know, but he has also assigned this area of his business portfolio to me. He expects me to handle it by myself."

"By yourself? Or with the help of his minions?"

"We are *familia*. His people are my people."

"Well, you'll be disappointed to know that my boyfriend is not my boyfriend. He won't be back for your satisfaction. You'll have to go back for him."

Andrés touched a hand to his nose. "Oh, he'll be back to find you. And when he does, I will take care of him. A man does not fight that fiercely for someone he does not love."

Sophia snorted. "Like you would know what love is."

"I have known love," Andrés said. "I have known the kind of love that you would move heaven and earth to keep alive. Your man loves you. He would move heaven and earth to come after you."

Sophia snorted.

The determined look on Andrés face sent a shiver of apprehension down Sophia's spine.

Blade had injured the man's ego. Andrés wouldn't let it go. He'd get his revenge and then he'd sell Sophia to the highest bidder.

Well, to hell with that. Sophia wasn't going to let him get away with either. She'd get the hell out of there before Blade found her and before Andrés could capture him.

CHAPTER 12

BLADE AND RAMÓN crept along the side of the dirt road until they reached the rutted path leading into the jungle. To the untrained eye, it looked like an impenetrable forest. And from a distance or from satellite, no one would know there was anything out there but jungle.

They were still about fifty yards away when Blade spotted movement. He put his hand out to stop Ramón. Blade pressed a finger to his lips to indicate silence. They ducked low in the foliage.

A man carrying an AK-47 leaned against a tree, his gaze on the road in front of him. He appeared bored.

As Blade studied the shadows, he spotted another man on the other side of the rutted path. He carried a submachine gun. And he too appeared bored as he kicked a rock.

Blade pointed in the direction that the rutted path led. They swung wide of the two men on guard at the entrance to the road leading into the jungle and moved through the trees and underbrush parallel to the rutted path.

A hundred yards in, they found a concrete wall, six feet high. Ramón cupped his hands and bent low. The only way to find out what was on the other side was to go over the wall. Blade stepped into the other man's palms.

Ramón straightened and lifted Blade off the ground.

Blade pulled himself up to the top of the wall, looking first before he committed. In front of him was a long building with very small windows. When he saw no movement on the back side or on either end of the wall, he straddled the wall then pushed to his feet and walked along the top of the wall like it was a balance beam.

When he arrived at the end of the long building, he dropped down and hugged the wall, creating as low a silhouette as he possibly could. Then he inched forward. Beyond the long narrow building was a larger one that looked like a fortified residence with few windows.

Buried in the jungle like it was, it was an excellent spot for a cartel stronghold and a perfect place to take Sophia.

He counted a guard at the front entrance of the

larger building and another peeking around the back corner.

Blade studied what he could, wishing he was Superman with X-ray vision to see inside the walls to find Sophia. After a while, he scooted backward until he was behind the barracks building.

He dropped down beside Ramón and motioned for them to make a full circle around the area, counting all the guards. When he returned, he didn't want any surprises.

Without help or weapons, he could do little to break into the compound. Blade had to recruit some help and do it in a hurry.

Ramón and Blade hurried back to where they'd ditched the motorcycles.

"What are you going to do?" Ramón asked.

Blade shook his head. "I don't know. I need help. At the very least, I need a distraction so that I can get past the guards and inside the compound."

"You can't do it alone," Ramón said.

"I don't have my team with me, so I'm on my own. I have to do something. I don't know what they'll do with Sophia."

Ramón led the way back to Cancún, pulling to the side of the road near the outskirts. Blade stopped beside him.

"I will help," Ramón said. "And I know friends and relatives who dislike the cartels as much as I do and are willing to do something about them."

"Do you know anybody with some C-4 or anything I can use to make a big bang? I feel like I need to blow a hole in the exterior wall as well as the interior wall. We'll need a distraction, because, once I get inside, it's going to take time to find Sophia. I might need a number of explosions just to get their attention away from inside the compound and bring the guards out."

Ramón nodded. "I have a cousin."

Blade almost smiled. "One who can hook me up with explosives?"

"The same one who gave us the coordinates."

"Maria's cousin?"

He dipped his head. "He is my cousin as well."

Ramón's cellphone buzzed. He glanced down at it. "It's Maria." He lifted it and pressed it to his ear. He listened for a minute and nodded. "Si." He ended the call and looked across at Blade. "The cartel left a message all over your bungalow. The resort staff are concerned."

"What was the message?"

"Surrender or she dies."

"That's it? No instructions on how I surrender?"

Ramón shook his head. "No. I expect that they will call or leave a message someplace else. For now, we will return to the resort. They know to find you there."

Blade revved the engine on his motorcycle, anger

burning through him. "We need to return the motorcycles to your cousin."

Ramón shook his head. "Not yet. You may have need of them later."

"Are we going straight back to the hotel, or do we need to ditch the motorcycles before we get there?"

"We might as well go back to the hotel and park in the employee parking lot. We can slip in through the back entrance."

They rode the motorcycles, zigzagging through the streets of Cancún back to the resort and parked in the rear. Darkness had settled in. It was getting late. Blade worried about what was happening with Sophia. He'd hated leaving the compound, but he knew he couldn't do anything on his own. He slipped around back of the bungalows. Ramón broke off and said that he would get back with him after he talked with his cousin.

Blade needed supplies, he needed explosives and he needed a bigger gun. Most of all, he needed his team.

When Blade arrived at the bungalow, he shined his flashlight from his cellphone at the building and cringed. Although it appeared as if someone had tried to scrub off the paint, there were still bold red letters spelling, *Surrender or she dies.* Footsteps behind him made him spin around. A familiar face appeared out of the darkness.

"Dude," Rucker said, "I like what you've done with the place."

A huge sense of relief washed over Blade as his friend and teammate engulfed him in a hug.

"How did you get here so fast? Is it just you?" Blade asked. "Because if it is, I can use all the help I can get, even if it's just one other guy."

"No, man, they wouldn't let me have all the fun." Rucker stood back with a grin.

"That's right. We couldn't let Rucker have all of the fun," Mac's voice said as he walked out of the shadows.

"No," Dawg said, following Mac. "You're stuck with the whole damned team."

The rest of the guys emerged from the shadows.

Blade laughed. "How the hell did you get everybody here so quickly?"

Rucker turned to Dash.

"Sunny had connections," Dash said. "One of her counterparts in the music industry has a private jet. She called in a favor, and he had his pilot transport us down here."

"Not only that, but we also got to skip customs," Rucker added.

Blade captured his gaze. "Does that mean...?"

Rucker nodded.

"Thank God." Blade hugged Rucker. "Please tell me you brought something that will make a big bang?"

Rucker smiled. "Will a couple pounds of C-4 be enough?"

Blade grinned. "If it's not, I might have a connection here."

"Do you know where they took her?" Rucker asked.

"I have a good idea. I performed a reconnaissance on it. It's out in the jungle and pretty heavily guarded."

Bull clapped his hands together. "Just the kind of challenge we need on vacation."

Blade frowned. "What did you tell the commander?"

"We told him we were all going on a fishing trip, and that we'd be out of cellphone range for at least a couple of days," Rucker said. "If he calls, don't answer."

"How'd you get hold of the weapons and the C-4?"

Rucker shook his head. "You know us. We all like our boy toys. We gathered up what we could, broke into your place and got your guns, and the C-4 was confiscated from a prior mission. Don't tell the commander. We'll all lose our jobs."

"Well, we better come up with a plan quickly." Blade shoved a hand through his hair. "I don't want them to move her while we're standing around patting each other on the back. I especially don't want them to know that my team is here. Let's get out there, form a plan and bust her out."

"That's right," Bull said. "Can't have the best bartender at the Salty Dog going missing."

"You guys got transport?" Blade asked.

Rucker nodded. "Sure do. We rented a nine-passenger van."

"That'll get us all out there." Blade waved toward the door. "Let's go inside. I'll draw out a map of the compound."

They crowded into the bungalow. Dawg let out a low whistle.

"Damn," Bull said.

"No kidding," Mac seconded.

Whoever had painted the outside had gone inside and tossed everything, including the furniture. Sofa cushions had been ripped, bedding shredded and their suitcases had been turned upside down. Clothes lay all over the place, some ripped, others spray painted.

"Looks like they did a little interior redecorating in here," Dash said.

Blade didn't give a damn about what had happened to the inside of the bungalow. Things could be replaced. People couldn't. All he cared about was coming up with a plan to rescue Sophia. He found a pen and piece of paper, laid it out on the counter and started drawing what he could remember of the compound. He indicated where the sentries stood guard on the exterior wall as well as on the interior buildings.

When a knock sounded at the door, all members of the team stiffened and turned toward the sound.

Blade touched a finger to his lips, and his team faded back into the shadows. He went to the door. "Who is it?"

"Ramón," came a muffled voice through the door panel.

Blade checked through the peephole.

Ramón stood outside.

Blade opened the door, stuck his head out and checked both right and left.

"I am alone," Ramón said. "I came in from the backside. I made certain no one followed me."

Blade pulled Ramón through the door and closed it quickly behind him, then he turned to his team. "Guys, this is Ramón. He and his cousins helped me find the compound."

The guys all moved forward out of the shadows into the light.

Rucker's eyes narrowed. "Can he be trusted?"

Ramón lifted his chin. "I hate what the cartel has done to our city. Even more so, I hate what the cartel has done to my family. They killed my brother, my mother and my father as they slept because they got the wrong address. They'd come in search of a member of a rival gang who actually lived next door."

"I'm sorry to hear that," Blade said.

Ramón nodded. "Working at the resort is my livelihood. It's what pays the bills to raise my two children and protect my wife. The people of Cancún are tired of being held hostage by the cartel. I will gladly assist you in any way to bring them down."

Rucker stepped forward. "You have to understand we're not here on official U.S. business. What we do here will have to remain anonymous. No one can know that members of the U.S. military were involved."

Ramón's mouth formed a tight line. "Then you need us even more."

Rucker tilted his head. "How so?"

"To give the credit to someone else for taking down the cartel."

Rucker shook his head. "We're not here to take down the cartel. We're here to rescue a U.S. citizen."

Ramón nodded. "I understand, but you are going into their compound. They will die defending it. There are those who track cartel members. Someone will have to take credit. I know just who those someones will be."

Rucker shot a glance toward Blade and back to Ramón. "Are you part of a rival gang?"

He shook his head. "We are not a part of a cartel. We are just concerned citizens who would like to clean up what the cartel has muddied. If you get it started, we'll finish it."

"Word cannot get out that we were here," Rucker

said. "It could create an international incident between the Mexican and the U.S. governments."

Ramón drew in a deep breath and let it out. "Understood."

"Okay," Rucker said with his eyes narrowed. "We're going in to get our citizen out. When we're done, it's up to you to take it from there." His jaw hardened. "Just don't get in the way."

Ramón waved a hand. "If you need additional firepower, we have it. Some of our members are former Mexican military special forces, including me and our cousin." Ramón met Blade's gaze.

Blade turned to Rucker. "Maria's cousin is also Ramón's cousin, and he was the one who gave us the coordinates to find the compound."

"Did you bring communications equipment?" Blade asked Rucker.

Rucker tipped his head toward Bull.

Bull nodded. "I have it all."

"How'd you get it past the commander?"

Bull shrugged. "Don't worry about it."

"Equip everybody, including Ramón," Rucker said. "Put Ramón on a different communication frequency. Blade you'll be in charge of notifying Ramón of what's going on."

The Deltas gathered around the small dining table while Blade and Ramón discussed the layout of the compound and the roads leading in.

"The best way we can use the people in Ramón's

group would be as the first line of defense on the roads coming in."

Ramón nodded. "We can do that."

Bull equipped Ramón with a headset with a specific frequency on it. He gave another headset to Blade with the same frequency. They tested them to make sure they worked.

After tucking the device into his pocket, Ramón's brow dipped. "Would it help if we could get somebody inside? Before you launch your attack?"

"Hell yeah, it would," Rucker said. "They could locate Sophia before we go in. That would help a lot."

Ramón glanced at Blade. "I think Maria can get in."

Blade shook his head. "How?"

"She had a relationship with one of the cartel members who happens to be one of Calderón's guards."

"I don't think it's a good idea," Rucker said.

"Me either," Blade agreed. "We don't want to put Maria in danger."

"She will be part of the team I'm working with." Ramón shrugged. "She offered. She doesn't want anything to happen to Miss Sophia either. Again, our jobs here at the resort are our livelihoods. What the cartel is doing is threatening our livelihoods. We want them gone."

"You know as soon as this gang is gone, another will replace them," Rucker said. "Money talks. Even good people with the best intentions are lured by money."

"If she wants in, let her," Dawg said. "At the very least she can locate Sophia and make it easier to find her when we get inside. She can also warn her about what's going to happen. And if we wait one more night, she might be able to tell us more about the compound."

Blade shook his head. "We can't wait another night. They might move her."

Rucker's eyes narrowed. "Have they tried to contact you yet?"

Blade's lips pressed together. "No."

"They want you to give yourself up, but they have to contact you in order to give you instructions on how to surrender."

"I don't want to wait until then," Blade said. "I want to take care of this before we get to that point. We don't know enough about the inside of that compound. Maria can get in and get back out with information that will give us a better idea of what we're up against."

Rucker's brow puckered. "We aren't absolutely certain they have Sophia there. Did you see her go in or come out?"

Blade shook his head. "But my gut tells me she's there."

"If we go in there and blow up the outer walls, and then blow up the interior structure's walls, we might take Sophia out with it. Or we might be knocking down some rich celebrity's home who wanted to have a place with absolute privacy."

Blade's lips pressed tightly together. They were right. They didn't know absolutely for sure that Sophia was inside that complex. All he had was coordinates from a man he didn't know, but who had delayed the cartel members from capturing him.

Blade's phone rang. He glanced down to see who was calling, but it was a "no caller" ID number. His pulse sped, and he glanced across at Rucker.

"Put it on speaker," Rucker said.

Blade answered immediately and put it on speaker. "This is Blade."

"If you want to see your woman again, you will meet me at the cathedral in downtown Cancún at midnight tomorrow night."

"How do I even know you have her?" Blade asked.

"Because we do."

"Let me talk to her," Blade demanded. "I want to know she's alive."

There was silence, and then he heard a yelp and a, "Stop pulling my hair you, son of a bitch!"

"Sophia!" Blade called out, "Sophia, are you doing okay, babe?"

She grunted. "I'd be doing a lot better if this asshole wasn't pulling my hair."

Blade couldn't help but grin. At least he knew she

was alive. "Tomorrow night midnight. I'll be there, but she better be there, too."

"Come alone," the voice said.

"Don't do it, Blade," Sophia called out. "They're just going to kill you."

"I'm coming to get you, Sophia," Blade said. "Hang tight."

"I can get myself out of this," she said. "It's my fault I'm here in the first place. Don't do it."

The call ended.

"Sophia!" Blade called out, but she was gone. He wanted to throw his cellphone, but he needed it in case they tried to get in touch with him again. He looked across at his team. "We have to get her out of there." He turned to Ramón. "If Maria's game, send her in, but gear her up with communications equipment. I don't know how she's going to get in there, but we need to know what's going on inside."

Ramón nodded. "Her ex-boyfriend has been after her to come back to them. She used to be a part of the group of cartel members, until she was almost busted by the Mexican police. She got a job at the resort and left the cartel behind."

Blade nodded. "Then she can get in and not raise too many eyebrows."

CHAPTER 13

AFTER THEY'D THROWN Sophia into the dark room, she'd spent the next hour feeling her way along the wall for anything sharp that she could use to tear the tape away from her wrists. The only thing protruding from any wall was the door handle, and it wasn't sharp enough to do anything.

With no way to free her wrists she sat on the floor and tried to think of another way to get free. Her only hope was that somebody would come in long enough for her to headbutt them hard enough to knock them flat on their ass and out cold. Then she might be able to run through the building and find something that she could use to break the tape on her wrists.

How plausible was that?

Exhausted from her struggle she must have fallen asleep. The next thing she knew the door opened and light flooded the room. She blinked as the two goons who had dragged her in there hurried in and grabbed her up by the arms and dragged her down the hall to what looked like a study, inside which she found Andrés Calderón talking on a cellphone.

He shoved the phone toward her at the same time one of the guards yanked her hair back. She cursed him.

A familiar voice called out, "Sophia!"

In the few short seconds she heard Blade's voice, hope blossomed in Sophia's chest, until Calderón cut off their conversation and ended the call.

Sophia had begged Blade not to come. Calderón would kill him. Then he'd do whatever he wanted with Sophia anyway. Whether that was to kill her or to sell her off to some sex trade, she didn't know, nor would she let it happen. She had to get herself out of the situation. She couldn't let Blade come alone to her rescue.

It would be suicide.

When the guards started to drag her back to her cell, she dug her feet into the floor. "No. Wait. I have to go to the bathroom. Andrés, tell them to take me to the bathroom. Surely you have such a thing in this compound. Or are you just a bunch of animals that piss out the door?"

"Take her back to her cell," he said.

"Fine. I'll pee all over your floor. Then you'll have to clean up after me," she shouted over her shoulder.

The guards dragged her toward her cell. Andrés called out in Spanish to them.

The two men holding her arms changed directions and shoved her inside a bathroom. Thankfully they closed the door, leaving her alone inside.

Unfortunately, there was no lock on the other side for her to lock them out. She quickly relieved herself while looking around the room for something, anything she could use as a weapon or to tear the tape.

She eyed a metal cabinet in the corner that had a sharp edge on the leg. She dropped to the floor, turned her back to the cabinet and scraped her wrists and the tape against the sharp metal leg. She didn't have much time. She had to cut through it quickly. She scraped hard, taking off skin as well as layers of tape.

After a minute or two, she could feel the tape loosening. She knew that if she pulled hard enough it would rip the rest of the way. Sophia staggered to her feet and used her foot to flush the toilet. Then she kicked the door. The guards opened it, grabbed her arms beneath her shoulders and led her back to her cell. Her wrists weren't free yet and those two goons were too much for her to handle by herself. She'd wait for another opportunity when her wrists were completely free. She might even try to see if she could open the door lock from the inside somehow. Maybe she could use the wiring in her swimsuit bra to jimmy the lock. Having her hands free would be a huge help.

Once inside her room with the door closed, she was plunged back into darkness. She turned her back to the door, hung her wrists on the doorknob and pulled hard. The rest of the tape snapped loose, and her wrists were free.

Sophia pulled the remaining tape off, taking a layer of skin with it. She quickly took her swimsuit top off and worked the underwire out of the bra. She dressed in the top sans the underwire and felt on the door handle until she found the little hole in the middle. She stuck the wire in the hole and worked with it for the next hour to no avail. Tired and hungry, she sank to the floor and prayed for a miracle.

She didn't wake until she heard the sound of footsteps in the hallway the next day. She assumed it was the next day. It was still dark as pitch in the room she was locked in. People were moving about the complex, their footsteps clumping loudly in the hallway outside her door.

She hoped that they would come and bring her some food so that she might have a chance to slip out when they came in. With no furniture inside the room, it would have to use her strength and wits to make the attack.

Footsteps paused in front of her door. The sound of the lock being turned gave her hope. She pushed to her feet and stood ready to plow into whoever stood on the other side.

The door opened. Two guards stood beside each other, blocking her path, each wielding a gun pointed in her direction.

She was willing to plow into them but not into their guns. They could prove to be trigger happy, shooting first and worrying about cleaning up the mess later. Still pointing their guns at her chest, they stood aside as a woman stepped through carrying a tray with a bowl and a piece of bread. The light behind her threw her face in the shadows.

She didn't speak as she stepped into the room, set the tray on the floor and backed away. When she looked up, she caught Sophia's gaze and gave her a slight nod. That's when Sophia recognized her.

Maria.

Sophia opened her mouth to say something.

Maria gave the slightest shake of her head.

Immediately, Sophia understood she did not want to out Maria.

Knowing there was a friendly face inside the compound helped Sophia. If she could get free of the room, Maria might help her find her way out.

The woman backed out of the room.

The two men with the guns continued to point at her until the door was closed firmly and locked behind them.

Sophia slumped. So much for a chance at escape.

But at least Maria was in the complex. How she'd gotten in, Sophia didn't know, but she was glad she was there.

Another thought hit her.

What if Maria had always been in cahoots with Andrés Calderón?

No. Sophia shook her head. The kind housekeeper couldn't be part of the cartel all along. If she had been, she would have smirked or shown some triumphant sign that she had duped Sophia.

No, Maria was there to help. Sophia had to believe that. Though, how could one woman help her get out of this iron tight compound? Sophia didn't know yet, but she'd figure it out. In the meantime, she had to fuel her body for when she did have a chance to escape. She might have to run a long way to get away from Andrés Calderón and his followers.

Sophia spent the next couple of hours thinking about what she would do if she got out of there. First thing she'd do was tell Blade how she felt about him. If that ruined their friendship so be it. She loved him. He needed to know.

She went over and over the kisses and making love with him. He had to have had so many more experienced women. How did she measure up? Since she couldn't see in the darkness, she closed her eyes and pictured lying in bed with Blade, his hands skimming across her body, his lips following. She wanted that again. She wanted to wake up next to him every day of her life. She loved spending time with him in his backyard grilling, drinking beer and talking about plans for their respective houses.

She wanted to plant a garden, he wanted to put up a basketball hoop. They talked about their friends and how they were so happy together. The women who had joined the men already seemed such an integral part of their group. They were there for each other when the guys deployed. Even Sunny Daye found time to come down to Killeen and join in a girls' night out when they were feeling lonely for their men.

They always ended up at the Salty Dog, which made it easy for Sophia to become part of the gang. She wasn't officially anybody's woman, but the team included her on weekends when they would grill out at other members of the team's homes. Blade would let her ride with him. Of course, they'd always been friends. What better way to love somebody than to start as friends?

Maybe that was why Blade never could commit to one woman. They weren't friends first.

Sophia sighed. Maybe she shouldn't tell him that she loved him. Maybe it was better to have him as a friend than not have him at all. Her chest ached with the amount of love she felt for him. She wanted more than anything to tell him that she loved him, but if it destroyed their friendship and he never wanted to see her again…

Well, she may have to rethink that. First, she had to get out of this hell hole. If she'd heard Calderón correctly as they dragged her into the room to speak to Blade on the phone, he had given the Delta a deadline. The cathedral in Cancún at midnight tonight. She only had a few short hours to escape to keep Blade from walking into a trap and giving Calderón the opportunity to torture and kill him.

WITH THE ULTIMATUM firmly in place, and Blade needing to be at the cathedral at midnight, they made the decision that he wouldn't be there. They had to get to the compound in the jungle before they moved Sophia. If the cartel even planned to move her. Blade really didn't think that they would show up with her in front of the cathedral. His gut told him that she was in that compound and she'd stay there until they found a buyer for her. He had to get there and get her out, first.

Dawg, being closest to the same height as Blade, had volunteered to take Blade's place at the rendezvous in Cancún. Mac would be his backup. They'd decided that Ramón and his group of Cancún vigilantes wouldn't be a part of the jungle compound takedown. They would go with Dawg and Mac and wait in hiding, ready to confront the cartel contingent who showed up.

With a group of the cartel members splitting off

to go to the downtown Cancún location, that would leave a smaller group to guard the complex out in the jungle.

Blade, Rucker, Dash, Bull, Tank and Lance would be out in the jungle ready to blow the compound wide open. They'd blow a hole in the exterior wall first to get the cartel's attention on that portion of the compound, drawing them away from the other end. They'd use C-4 in a small amount on the doors at the front and back of the complex to breach the main building. They'd also use some C-4 to damage the long barracks-like building. With all the explosions they hoped the confusion would keep the cartel busy while they got inside, found Sophia and got her out. With Maria inside they hoped that she could get to Sophia and warn her, maybe even get her moving out as they breached the interior complex.

With the largest portion of the Deltas headed out to the jungle in the rented van, Blade insisted on riding the borrowed motorcycle. He didn't like being confined inside the van.

Dawg and Mac went with Ramón into Cancún where they would recon the square and position Ramón's team to provide backup well before the appointed time. Ramón and Maria's cousin had gathered a group of ten vigilantes, each armed and ready to take on the cartel.

Blade hoped that they got through with the jungle complex and back to Cancún before the rendezvous time at midnight. He also hoped that communication didn't happen between the two groups of cartel members. The first thing they needed to do at the jungle location was cut the communication capabilities. That would mean destroying the communications tower at the center of the jungle complex. Lance was assigned to that task, while Blade would be inside with Rucker searching the rooms for Sophia. He expected that Andrés Calderón would be with the group headed into Cancún for his assignation in front of the cathedral.

Blade and his team parked over a mile away from the compound and moved in well before dark. They thoroughly tested their communications devices and kept in contact even as they spread out for surveillance of the site.

The two guards were still at the front entrance of the wall, but they only counted one at the rear, none on the sides, which made it easier for the Delta's to move in when the time was right.

Rucker and Blade had their eye on the front of the building where they positioned themselves before dusk. Darkness settled in early in the jungle, which made for a long wait until they finally saw vehicles leaving the complex.

Three trucks left with armed men inside, followed by a dark SUV. As soon as the vehicles cleared the compound and headed out onto the dirt road, Blade heard a crackling sound in his headset.

"La Señorita Sophia está aquí," came Maria's voice.

Blade drew in a deep breath and let go of a tiny bit of the tension that had been drawing him as tight as a bow. "Sophia's still inside," he translated for the others to hear. His gut had been right, and they had left without her, which meant that they'd no intention of exchanging her for him. The question was how heavily armed were they inside the compound?

Maria's voice came across again. *"Gran edificio. Pasillo largo. Última habitación a la izquierda."* The static almost made the message unintelligible.

Blade glanced in Rucker's direction, although he couldn't see him in the dark, and translated, "Large building. Long corridor. Last room on the left. Did you get that Rucker?."

Rucker sounded off, "Large building. Long corridor. Last room on the left. Got it."

They had a location. All they had to do was get inside. With the main group gone, that left the compound with at least eight guards fewer inside and out.

"Steady," Rucker warned. "Give them a few minutes to get down the road far enough."

Blade was like a horse champing at the bit. He wanted to get inside immediately and free Sophia. She was there. Mere yards away. But they had to go according to plan, take out the communications and create a distraction so they could get inside.

Fifteen minutes after the vehicles had left the

compound, Rucker came across on the headset. "All right, let's do this."

Bull and Dash had the backside of the compound.

A moment later Bull's voice came across. "Back guard down." Dash would set the C-4 compound on the back wall.

In the meantime, Rucker closed the distance to Blade as they approached the exterior wall. Rucker bent, cupped his hands, and helped Blade scale the wall.

Once on top, Blade surveyed. "All clear," he whispered back to Rucker and reached down to help Rucker scale the wall as well. Once inside Blade whispered into his mic. "Inside the wall."

Rucker placed a charge on the long barracks-like building and set the detonator. They moved on to the end of that building and looked both ways before approaching the main structure.

The two guards at the front entrance faced the gate talking quietly amongst themselves. Blade slipped around the back of the main building where a guard stood at the back door. When the man turned away from him, Blade slipped on silent feet and dispatched the guard quietly. "Back door guard down," he reported.

Rucker was supposed to set a charge on the front of the building at the same time that Blade applied a charge to the backdoor lock, just enough to break it free but not to blow the door away. Hopefully that door was at the long end of that hallway that Maria had talked about and that Sophia would be in the room near the end closest to him. But the building was large. The long hallway could be anywhere. He had to be ready to move fast. With his AR15 set on semiautomatic and his handgun on his hip, he stepped away from the back door and around the side of the building waiting for the explosions to begin.

"In T minus three seconds," Rucker said.

With his hands pressed to his ears, Blade counted down in his head, 3…2…1.

Blade pressed his detonator. The explosion on the back wall sent concrete chunks and dust particles flying through the air. Thankfully Blade had his hands over his ears to lessen the concussion impact. As soon as the dust cleared enough, he moved to the back door. The C-4 on the lock had done the trick. The door stood open. "Breaching the rear," Blade said into his headset.

"Down two guards in the front," Rucker reported. He and Dash would move in from the front entrance. Once the others cleared the exterior and the interior yards as well as the barracks building, they'd follow Rucker and Dash into the large structure.

The Deltas were to locate Sophia and Maria and get them both out of the building, preferably alive.

CHAPTER 14

SOPHIA HEARD the explosions and felt the ground shake beneath her. She pushed to her feet, felt her way to the door, grabbed the handle, and shook it. The lock held it in place. Something was happening out there. She was stuck inside.

As she stood there, the handle turned beneath her fingertips and the door pushed open. Prepared to bowl over whoever was standing on the other side, Sophia braced herself.

Maria's face appeared through the crack in the door. She waved for Sophia to follow her.

Sophia dove through the opening and blinked in the first light she'd seen in hours. As they started down the corridor, the two men who'd dragged Sophia into her cell burst from a room headed toward her.

Sophia screamed for effect, ducked low and charged like a linebacker on a football team. Two steps behind her Maria did the same. The men didn't have time to lift their weapons and aim at them.

The women hit the men in the gut, knocking them backward. They staggered but they didn't fall.

The one Sophia hit grabbed her arms and used her to steady himself.

She reached for the butt of his weapon and slammed it upward, hitting him in the jaw. Then she kneed him in the groin. When he doubled over, she thrust her palm up sharply, hitting his nose.

The man yelled and grabbed for his face as blood gushed from his nose.

Maria wasn't having as much luck. Sophia grabbed for her guy's weapon, but she couldn't break it from his grip. She got her finger in the trigger, jammed the barrel into the other man's belly and pulled.

The man holding Maria grunted and slumped forward, releasing his grip on the other woman.

Maria ducked past him and raced down the corridor.

As she tried to run past her guard, Sophia was pulled up short when her guard grabbed a handful of her hair and yanked her backward. Holding her hair in one hand, he raised his weapon with the other and pointed it at her chin.

Damn, this couldn't be it, Sophia thought. She'd made it too far to have her head blown away. Just as that thought whizzed through her mind, the guard's hand on her arm loosened, his eyes widened, and he slumped, falling to the floor at her feet.

Blade stood behind him, removing the knife out of the guard's neck. He grabbed Sophia, pulled her against him, crushed her lips with his, and then broke free. "Come with me if you want to live."

"Seriously?" Sophia laughed. "You're going to quote a movie?" She moved with him, running down a corridor. Maria had reached the other end where Rucker stood over the body of another guard. As they passed the room that Sophia recognized as Calderón's study an older man, who looked very much like Andrés, stepped out, a submachine gun in his hands. He reached out and grabbed Sophia as she was running by and yanked her up against his body.

"Dammit, I cleared that room!" Blade cursed.

Calderón gave a wicked grin. "I have a secret door. Only those who know where it is can find it. Put down your weapons or I'll kill her." He pointed the submachine gun at her head.

Sophia couldn't believe it. She had come this far. Blade had kissed her. Now she was caught again. "Bullshit on this." She rammed her elbow into the man's gut and ducked her head as the machine gun went off. Sophia grabbed his arm and spun around behind him. The elder Calderón still had control of the machine gun and was firing into the corridor.

Blade, Rucker, and Maria all hit the ground. The man wasn't aiming. He was firing at random, as Sophia pulled his arm up hard behind his back.

"Let go or I'll break your arm," she said.

He didn't drop the weapon. He stood on his toes and kept firing. Then a loud bang sounded from where Blade lay on the floor.

The elder Calderón stopped firing and stood still for a moment. Then he lurched forward and fell on his face. Still holding his arm, Sophia almost went down with him. She let go before she did.

Blade stood and pulled Sophia into his arms. Rucker helped Maria to her feet.

Lance, Tank, Bull and Dash entered the building and found them in the corridor.

"All clear in the barracks and outside," Tank reported.

"Good work," Rucker said.

Blade turned to Lance. "Did the communication tower come down?"

Lance nodded. "It did."

"Hopefully no communications got out," Blade said.

"Blade, you stay with the women. We'll doublecheck all the rooms inside this building," Rucker said.

"Roger."

The five men went from room to room checking all closets, beneath the beds and anywhere a man could hide. When they returned, Rucker said, "All clear."

Blade's jaw tightened. "Let's get to the cathedral. I have a bone to pick with Andrés Calderón."

The men headed out of the compound.

Before he left, the corridor, Blade held Sophia in his arms and whispered into her ear, "In case I haven't told you, I love you."

She clung to him for a brief moment and whispered back, "It's a good thing, because I love you too. Screw the friend zone."

He laughed and took her hand, and they left the building.

Sophia rode back to Cancún on the back of the motorcycle with Blade. He'd insisted that she wear the helmet. She wrapped her arms tightly around his middle, loving every second of their closeness and basking in the fact that he'd said he loved her.

Wow. Sophia's heart sang.

What had changed his mind? Or had he not changed his mind about commitment, but he still loved her? She didn't care; she was free from the cartel's clutches. Whatever kind of love Blade wanted to give her, she was damn well happy to get it.

They arrived in Cancún near midnight. As soon

as they were within radio range, Blade contacted Dawg and arranged a meeting place where he would take Dawg's place, and then the Deltas would take positions around the square near the cathedral.

"I need someone to make sure Maria and Sophia are taken care of," Blade said.

"I can take—" Sophia started.

"—take care of yourself," Blade, Rucker, Dash, Mac, Dawg, Tank, Lance and Bull all said at once, and then laughed.

"We know you can take care of yourself," Blade said. "To Andrés Calderón you're nothing but a pawn in this game. If he captures you again, that puts all of us at risk."

Sophia crossed her arms over her chest. "I get that, but you're a pawn, too. He wants you, and he'll do anything to get you. So, don't be an idiot and get yourself killed."

Blade pulled her close to him. "No way. We've got something going here, and I'm not ready to give it up."

She frowned. "If you plan on giving it up, you might as well do it now. I plan on playing for keeps."

He kissed her hard on the lips. "Good, because apparently I do, too. When I find the right one. And you, my dear, are the right one."

The Delta team members all grinned.

"Come on, let's take care of business," Rucker said. "Dawg, let Ramón's team know not to shoot us."

"Already did," Dawg said.

"Bull, Dash and Lance," Rucker pointed to each one of them, "you're on the women. Don't let them out of your sight and protect them with your lives."

The three men popped a salute and moved in to surround Maria and Sophia.

"I'd rather you gave me a gun," Sophia said. "I'll shoot that bastard myself."

Blade shook his head with a grin. "Remind me not to make you mad."

She narrowed her eyes. "That's right. Don't make me mad. You have to sleep sometime."

"As long as it's with you, babe, I'll die a happy camper." He kissed the tip of her nose then claimed her lips.

"Just don't die today," she said. And she wrapped her arms around his neck and pulled him down to kiss him again. "I mean it. Don't die today."

He winked. "Yes, ma'am."

Dawg looked up from his watch. "Clock's about to strike midnight."

Rucker nodded. "We need Cinderella out in front of the pumpkin."

Blade nodded. "On my way."

Sophia watched him as he climbed into the van that had transported the team to the square. Her chest tightened as he shut the door and started the engine. The plan was to use the van as a shield against whatever bullets might fly his way. Sophia knew better. The metal on the vehicle wouldn't stop bullets. She prayed it didn't come to an all-out war. Blade wouldn't stand a chance.

The team spread out, surrounding Blade's position.

What killed Sophia was that Blade didn't have to go. The team had rescued her and Maria from the complex in the jungle. "Why is he doing this?" she whispered.

Bull stared out after Blade. "If he doesn't, Calderón will still be a threat."

"Then we'll just go back to the States. Calderón won't follow us there. Screw this game of bait and switch."

"Ramón and the good people of Cancún deserve closure," Dash said.

Lance nodded. "Until they get the leaders of the cartel, it won't be over."

Near to tears, Sophia swallowed hard. "But why does Blade have to be the target?"

"He really doesn't have to be, but he wants to take care of Andrés Calderón as much as Ramón's people do," Bull said. "The people of Cancún are tired of the cartel demanding payola and disturbing the tourists who provide their livelihood."

Blade drove the van out to the center of the square in front of the cathedral. As far as Sophia could tell, the square was empty, except for Blade and the van. The Delta team and Ramón's people hid in the shadows, ready to take on the cartel.

Sophia didn't know what to expect, but when three truckloads of armed men raced into the square, her breath caught and held in her throat. She pressed her fingers against her lips and watched in terror.

A dark SUV followed the three big trucks. The trucks surrounded the rented van.

Sophia turned to Bull. "Give me your handgun. Please. You have to go help Blade." She could tell by the way Bull and the other two were standing that they wanted to help.

Bull shook his head, his jaw tense. "No. Blade told us to take care of you."

"Give me a gun," she pleaded. "I'll take care of us. Blade needs his team now." When Bull, Lance and Dash refused to move, Sophia stomped her foot. "If you guys don't go, I will." She pushed past Bull and headed for Blade, the van and the cartel's trucks.

Bull snagged her around the middle and pulled her back into the shadows. He handed her a pistol, showed her how to use it, and then he said, "Please don't shoot us."

"I know how to fire a pistol. Sarge taught me everything he knows." She gripped the pistol in one hand and shoved Bull with the other. "Go."

"Just stay here," Bull said to Sophia then nodded to the other two men. They took off across the pavement.

The men in the trucks opened fire on the van with semiautomatic weapons and submachine guns, and they kept firing.

Sophia's heart leaped into her throat, and her world stood still as the horror unfolded.

The Deltas moved in and picked off the gunmen, one at a time, until the last one threw down his weapon and held his hands high.

Her attention on the van, and her concern for Blade, were Sophia's downfall.

Behind her, Maria squealed.

Sophia spun with the gun in her hand.

Andrés Calderón held a handgun to Maria's head. "I'll make a trade with you," he said. "Your life for hers."

She aimed her pistol at Andrés head. "How about I just shoot you and end this now?"

He snorted, his lip curling back in a snarl. "Who will pull the trigger first? You'd sacrifice Maria's life for yours? That doesn't sound like the kind of person I thought you were."

Sophia's eyes narrowed. "You have no idea what kind of person I am, but I know what kind you are. You're an animal. Life doesn't mean much to you unless it's your own."

"Your life or hers," he said, his tone low and dangerous.

Sophia drew in a breath and let it go. She wanted

to kill the man, but he might kill Maria first. The woman had done so much for her; Sophia couldn't let her die. "Okay," she said. "We trade. But you have to let her go first."

Calderón shook his head. "No. Throw down your gun."

Sophia's jaw hardened. "I don't trust you. Take the barrel of your weapon away from Maria's head. Then I'll throw down mine."

His eyes narrowed to a squint. "I don't trust you. I guess that puts us at a standoff."

Maria's gaze captured Sophia's in the dim glow from a streetlight.

Sophia could tell her body was tensing. She was going to make a move. Sophia had to be ready.

Maria jammed her elbow into Calderón's gut and ducked her head away from the barrel of his gun.

He fired off a round, missing the housekeeper completely.

At the same time, Sophia pulled the trigger aiming for Calderón's chest. The bullet hit dead center. Sarge's lessons had paid off.

Calderón's eyes widened. His grip on his captive loosened.

Maria ran several steps away.

Calderón stared down at the hole in his chest and clutched it with his empty hand. He raised his weapon and aimed it at Sophia. Before Sophia could fire off another round, a loud bang sounded. Expecting pain, Sophia was surprised when she didn't feel any. Calderón had been aiming right for her.

The cartel leader fell to his knees, his gun slipping from his fingers. He toppled forward, face-first on the pavement. The man had two exit wounds on his back. Sophia spun to see who had fired the shot.

Blade hurried up beside her, carrying a semi-automatic rifle. "Are you all right?"

She nodded. "I am, now that I know you're all right."

He slung the strap over his shoulder and pulled her into his arms. "I think I just lost a few years off my life. I thought for sure he'd shoot you."

She wrapped her arms around his back still holding onto the pistol. "How did you survive those men shooting at you? I thought you were dead."

"I knew they were coming in three trucks. I figured that they would surround me. I figured Calderón was out for blood and would have given them orders to shoot to kill.

"As soon as I parked in the square, I slipped out of the van and lay beneath the chassis. They directed their bullets into the van where I would've been sitting." He leaned back, his lips pressing together. "They missed me, but my team didn't miss them."

Rucker, Mac, Bull and the rest of them gathered around Sophia and Blade.

Blade turned to Rucker. "What about the rest of the cartel? Any survivors besides the one who surrendered?"

"Ramón and his people will take care of them." Rucker nodded and turned toward the three trucks and the destroyed van where Ramón's people were collecting the survivors. He turned back to the Deltas. "We need to bug out before the Mexican police arrive on scene. Remember, we're not supposed to be here. We're supposed to be on a fishing trip."

Blade nodded. "And Sophia and I are supposed to be on vacation."

"I think we can manage all of that," Rucker said with a grin. "And I don't think we'll have any more trouble from the cartel. We took out the leaders. The Calderóns are no more."

"Good," Blade said. "Let's get back to the resort and see if they have any extra rooms for you guys."

"Dibs on a bungalow for us," Sophia added.

"Preferably one that isn't decorated in red spray paint," Blade said.

"What about the van?" Dawg asked. "We rented it. It'll link us to the scene."

"We'll report it as stolen," Rucker said.

Ramón appeared. "My people are thankful for what you and your team did for us. Please, let us give you a ride back to the resort."

"Do you have enough room in your vehicle?" Rucker asked.

Ramón smiled. "I have cousins."

EPILOGUE

"I'M SO glad we can finally relax." Sophia stood in the circle of Blade's arms, both up to their necks in one of the five swimming pools on the resort. She held a Mai Tai in her hands, while Blade held a beer.

Blade's arm circled her around her middle. "Me, too. This is the vacation I envisioned when you invited me along."

"Actually, this is exactly what I'd hoped for, except for the little issue of a kidnapping and a run-in with a deadly cartel." Sophia smiled. "Fortunately, we still have a few more days of sun, sand and water."

"And each other," Blade added.

Her cheeks heated. They'd gone way past the friend zone into the land of lovers since they'd arrived in Mexico. And the way Blade was talking, they'd be together long after they returned to the States. Sophia couldn't be happier.

The Deltas had also secured rooms at the resort, and each had gotten a drink from the bar and converged on the same pool with Blade and Sophia.

Dash held up his beer. "Here's to another successful mission."

Rucker frowned at him. "We weren't here on a mission."

Dash grinned. "But I caught the biggest fish."

"Quit bragging, douchebag," Dawg said.

Dash's grin widened. "You're just jealous because you had the smallest fish."

The guys had spent the day out on a chartered fishing boat. Blade had stayed behind with Sophia, though she'd insisted she'd be all right on her own.

She had wanted him to go out with the guys and enjoy the fishing, knowing they would have a blast. She'd needed the time for a secret task she'd wanted to complete. Since he'd stayed, she'd had to sneak away from Blade to make it happen. And if her timing was right, her plan would be revealed within the next thirty minutes.

"Well then, if we can't drink to a mission," Dash said, "then we should drink to our women. They should be here enjoying the fun in the sun with us."

"We thought so, too," said a feminine voice behind Sophia.

All the Delta's turned as one. Sunny Daye led the pack of women, including Nora Michaels, Kylie Adams, Layla Grey and Beth Drennan.

Nora wore a black string bikini. She carried a colorful drink in one hand and a towel in the other. "We couldn't let you guys have all the fun."

Rucker pulled himself up on the side of the pool and set down his beer. He stood, gathered Nora into his arms and kissed her soundly. "How did y'all get here?"

She laughed and turned to Sunny. "The same way you guys did. Sunny's got some connections."

Sunny's cheeks reddened. "I've made a few friends in the industry, and I just happen to have one who owns a plane. While you guys were out fishing, the pilot flew the aircraft back to the States to bring us to Cancún."

"Remind me to thank your friend," Rucker said as he held Nora in his arms.

Mac got out of the pool and hugged Kylie. "What strings did you have to pull to get time off to come down here?"

She shook her head. "You have no idea, but, damn it, I made it. I was determined to get some sun in the sand with my number one guy."

"Same here." Layla dropped her towel on a lounger, slid into the pool and swam over to where Bull was heading toward her. "I could use a little R&R with my guy."

The women all slipped into the pool, drinks in hand.

Dawg laid back, floating, looking up at the sky.

"Now, this is what I call a vacation."

Beth Drennan splashed water on him. "It seems a little bit tame for you, Dawg."

He lowered his legs and stood with a shrug. "Yeah, you're right. I might want to go out on the beach and see if I can get a little wave action. Anybody up for that? I know where I can get a boogie board."

"I'm in," Beth said.

"Me too," Tank said.

"And me," Lance echoed.

"You single guys, don't go flirting with any cartel members or Russian mobsters. I'd like to enjoy the rest of this vacation," Blade said. "I've got some catching up to do in the commitment arena."

"I thought you were a confirmed bachelor?" Rucker said.

Blade nodded, pulling Sophia close to him. "I was, until I realized how much I was in love with my friend and neighbor."

Dash snorted. "Took you long enough to figure it out."

"Tell me about it," Sophia agreed.

"The rest of us saw it coming," Mac said. "We couldn't fathom why you were so clueless."

"Hey, at least I figured it out before it was too late." Blade leaned his forehead against Sophia's. "The thought of losing you brought me to my senses."

"So, you gonna commit to one female?" Dawg asked.

Blade nodded, his gaze locking with Sophia's. "I am. As long as she'll have me."

Sophia nodded. "That's what I've always wanted."

"Really?" Blade's brow wrinkled. "Why didn't you ever say so?"

She snorted. "You had such a phobia about commitment, I wasn't going to screw up our friendship. If I couldn't have you all to myself, I was going to be content in the friend zone."

Blade shook his head. "Screw the friend zone. I want you all to myself."

She frowned, "You gotta understand it goes both ways."

He nodded, solemnly. "I understand, and I'm glad, because you're going to be my one and only."

"Mmm. I like the way that sounds," she said. "You wanna kiss on that?"

He lifted his chin and stared down at her, his face serious. "After you promise to marry me."

Sophia's heart fluttered and she blinked. "What?"

"You heard me," he said with a grin. "Will you marry me?"

Rucker laughed. "Damn, dude, when you make up your mind, you make up your mind."

"Yes, I do." Blade's gaze never wavered from Sophia's. "So, Sophia, will you marry me?"

Sophia stared into his eyes, happiness bubbling up in her chest. "Damn right, I will."

SEAL SALVATION

BROTHERHOOD PROTECTORS COLORADO
BOOK #1

New York Times & USA Today
Bestselling Author

ELLE JAMES

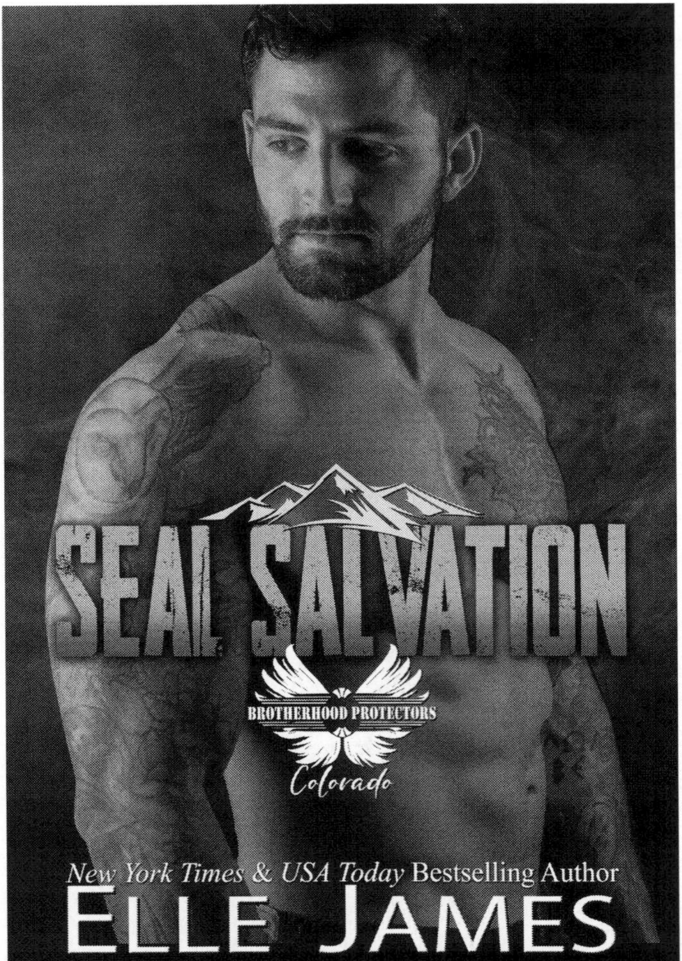
SEAL SALVATION
BROTHERHOOD PROTECTORS
Colorado
New York Times & USA Today Bestselling Author
ELLE JAMES

CHAPTER 1

JAKE COGBURN SAT in the tattered lounge chair he'd scavenged on the side of the street after moving into an empty apartment in Colorado Springs. He hadn't planned on living in an apartment, nor had he planned on sleeping on the only piece of furniture he could afford without digging into his savings. He'd put aside money to purchase a plot of land out in the middle of nowhere Colorado. On that land, he'd wanted to build a house.

All those plans had been blown away, along with the lower half of his left leg, when he'd stepped on an IED in Afghanistan. Yeah, he had the money in the bank, but what good did it do him? On one leg, what could he accomplish? Working a piece of land and building a house took all four limbs.

He poured another tumbler of whiskey and tipped the contents up, letting the cool liquid burn a path down his throat. Soon, the numbing effect set in. Jake could almost forget the phantom pain in his missing leg, could almost forget he'd not only lost a leg, but had lost the only family he'd ever had.

As a Navy SEAL, his teammates had been his brothers. Every one of them would lay down his life for him, as he'd taken one for the team when his foot had landed on that IED.

Medically discharged, having gone through multiple surgeries and physical therapy, he'd been dumped out into a civilian world that had no use for a one-legged, former Navy SEAL.

What was he good for? His skillset included demolitions, tactical operations, highly effective weapons firing and hand-to-hand combat.

Where could he find that kind of work in a civilian occupation? And doing all that balanced on one leg?

Nope.

He was all washed up. His only hope was to sit on a corner with his hat held out, begging like a hundred other homeless veterans roaming the streets of Colorado Springs.

His free hand clenched into a fist. Jake had never begged for anything in his life. He'd fought for what he'd accomplished. From surviving the gangs on the streets of Denver, to forging his way through BUD/S training, he'd always counted on his mind and brute strength to get through any hardship.

But now…

Through the empty glass tumbler, he stared down at the stump below his left knee then slammed the glass against the wall. It hit hard and shattered into a million pieces that scattered across the floor.

A knock sounded on the door to his apartment.

"I didn't put a dent in the damned wall!" he yelled. "Leave me the fuck alone."

"Jake Cogburn?" An unfamiliar male voice called out from the other side of the faded wooden panel.

"Yeah," Jake muttered. "I'm not interested in buying anything."

"I'm not selling anything," the muffled voice sounded.

"Then get the fuck away from my door," Jake said and tipped the bottle of whiskey up, downing the last swallow. The bottle followed the glass, hitting the wall with a solid thump before it crashed to the wooden floor and bounced.

"Everything all right in there?" the man called out.

"Who the hell cares?" Jake muttered.

"I do."

Jake frowned. "I told you. I'm not buying anything."

"And I told you I'm not selling anything." A moment of silence followed. "Would you open the door for a brother?"

Anger surged through Jake. "I don't have a brother. I'm an only fuckin' child."

"Then how about a brother-in-arms? A fellow spec ops guy? A Delta Force man?"

Jake barked a single laugh. "Yeah. Yeah. Whatever. The SEALs don't operate out of Colorado. And as far as I know, there isn't a Delta Force unit near here."

"Not active Delta Force," the man fired back. "Look. A friend sent me to offer you a job."

"I don't have any friends," Jake said, then added muttering beneath his breath, "and I'm not fit for any jobs."

"You're fit for the job he's got in mind," the man said. "Look, Cog, the only easy day was yesterday. Are you a SEAL or not?"

Cog.

Only the men he'd fought with side by side had called him Cog.

A frown pulled his brow low as he leaned forward in his chair. "Anyone can look up the SEAL motto. How do I know you're the real deal?" Jake had to admit he was curious now.

"You have to trust me." The man chuckled. "It's not like us Deltas have tridents tattooed on our foreheads like you Navy SEALs. My honor was forged in battle, just like yours."

Despite himself, Jake's lips twitched. No, they didn't have tridents, the symbol of their trade, drawn in indelible ink on their foreheads. But it was etched into their hearts. The grueling training they'd survived had made them proud to wear the symbol of the Navy SEAL and even prouder to fight as a team alongside the Delta Force operatives.

"Who sent you?" Jake asked.

"Hank Patterson," the voice said and waited.

A flood of memories washed over Jake. Hank had been his mentor when he'd come on board, fresh from BUD/S training. He hadn't hazed him as the others on the team had. He'd taken Jake beneath his wing and taught him everything he knew that would help him in the many missions to come. Many of Hank's techniques had kept Jake alive on more than one occasion. He owed the man his life.

"Why didn't Hank come himself?" Jake asked.

"He and his wife have a new baby. You might not be aware that his wife is a famous actress. She's going on set in a few days, and Hank has diaper duty."

"Hank? Diaper duty?" Jake shook his head. The alcohol in his system made his vision blur. "Doesn't sound like Hank."

"Well, it is. Will you open the door so we can discuss his proposition?"

Jake glanced around the pathetic excuse of an apartment and shook his head. "No. But I'll come out in a minute. You can buy me a drink, and we can talk."

"Good," the man said. "Anything to get out of this hallway. Your neighbors are giving me threatening looks."

Jake reached for his prosthesis, pulled up his

pantleg, donned the inner sleeve, slipped his stump into position and pulled the outer sleeve over his thigh. He slid his good foot into a shoe and pushed to a standing position, swaying slightly.

He smelled like dirty clothes and alcohol. But he'd be damned if he let Hank's emissary into the apartment to see how low Jake Cogburn had sunk.

Lifting his shirt up to his nose, he grimaced. Then he yanked it over his head, slung it across the room and reached into the duffel bag in the corner for another T-shirt.

The sniff test had him flinging that shirt across the room to land with the other in a heap on the floor. Two shirts later, he settled on a black Led Zeppelin T-shirt that had been a gift from one of his buddies on his last SEAL team. The man had been a fan of one of the biggest bands of the seventies, a time way before he'd been born.

Running a hand through his hair, he shoved his socked-foot and his prosthetic foot into a pair of boots and finally opened the door.

The man on the other side leaned against the opposite wall in the hallway. He pushed away from the wall and held out his hand. "Jake Cogburn, I'm Joseph Kuntz. My friends call me Kujo."

Jake gave the man a narrow-eyed glare but took the hand. "What kind of job does Hank have in mind. Not that I'm interested." He shook the hand and let go quickly.

"He's started a business up in Montana and wants to open up a branch here in Colorado." Kujo ran his glance over Jake.

Jake's shoulders automatically squared. "And?"

"And he wants you to head it up."

Jake laughed out loud. "Hank wants this broken-down SEAL to head up an office?"

Kujo nodded. "He does."

"Why don't *you* do it?"

"I have a pregnant wife back in Montana. I only have a few weeks to help you lay the groundwork. Then I have to get back."

His head shaking back and forth, Jake stared at the man as if he'd lost his mind. "What the hell kind of business can a one-legged ex-SEAL manage? Does he even know me?"

"He said he mentored you as a newbie SEAL a long time back. He knows your service record and thinks you would make the perfect man to lead the new branch." Kujo crossed his arms over his chest. "He has confidence that you have the skills needed to do the job. And there's no such thing as an ex-SEAL. Once a SEAL, always a SEAL. "

Jake nodded. The man was right. "He knew me back then. But does he know me now?" Jake touched the thigh of his injured leg.

Kujo nodded. "He knows about your circumstances, and he's still certain you're the one to do the job."

Jake shook his head. "What exactly will this branch of his business sell?"

"We're a service organization. We provide security and unique skills to our clients to protect them and/or take care of situations law enforcement or the military might not be in a position to assist with."

"Vigilantes?" Kujo held up his hands. "No thanks."

"Not vigilantes," Kujo said. "More a security service for those in need of highly trained special ops folks who know how to handle a gun and run a tactical mission."

"Again," Jake said, "sounds like vigilantes. No thanks. Besides, I'm not fit to fight. The Navy told me so." He turned to go back into his apartment and find another whiskey glass.

Kujo stepped between him and the door. "Can you fire a weapon?"

Jake shrugged. "Sure. Nothing wrong with my hands and arms. But I can't run, jump and maneuver the way I used to before..." He tipped his chin toward his prosthesis.

"You still have a brain. You can compensate," Kujo raised his eyebrows. "Do you have a job?"

Jake's chest tightened. "No."

Kujo's chin lifted a fraction. "Then, what do you have to lose?" He stood with his shoulders back, his head held high—the way Jake used to stand.

What did he have to lose? He'd lost everything that had been important to him. He couldn't sink any lower. His brows furrowing, he stared into Kujo's open, friendly face and then shrugged. "I have nothing to lose."

Kujo nodded. "Trust me. I've been there. Hank Patterson brought me out of the hell I'd sunk into. Life has only gotten better since."

"Well, you have both legs," Jake pointed out.

"And you have your hands and mind, one perfectly good leg and a prosthetic device you can get around on just fine from what I can see." He frowned. "Are you going to stand around bellyaching or come with me and start a new job I think you'll love."

"I'm not bellyaching," Jake grumbled.

"But you're wasting daylight, and I have another place I need to be before dark." Kujo stood back. "What's it to be?"

For a tense moment, Jake stood fast. After weeks of wallowing in the hovel of an apartment, getting out seemed more difficult than staying with the familiar.

"Why did Hank choose me?" he asked.

"Based on your past performance as a Navy SEAL, Hank thought you were the right person for the task he had in mind. He trusts you, your work and your integrity. The job won't always be easy…" Kujo grinned. "But the only easy day…"

"Yeah, yeah…was yesterday." Jake impatiently waved Kujo ahead of him. "I'm coming. But don't take that as a yes. I have yet to decide whether I want to work for Hank."

Kujo cocked an eyebrow. "You have a better job offer?"

Jake wanted to tell the man that he did, but he couldn't. "No."

"Fine. Come with me. We have another stop to make before we seal this deal and kick off this project." Kujo nodded toward the interior of the apartment. "Got a go bag?"

Jake glanced back. "Not since I left the service. Why?"

"We'll most likely stay the night where we're going. Maybe longer. Grab what you need for a couple of days."

Jake returned to his apartment, grabbed the duffel bag out of the bottom of the closet and stuffed a pair of jeans, socks, underwear, some T-shirts, a jacket and his shaving kit into it. He returned to his apartment entrance where Kujo waited.

The other man stepped outside and waited for Jake to follow.

Jake carried his bag through the door and pulled it closed behind him. "Where are we going?"

"To a ranch."

His feet coming to an immediate halt, Jake shook his head. "Why are we going to a ranch? You didn't say anything about a ranch."

Kujo drew in a deep breath and let it go slowly, as

if he was holding back his own impatience. "Bear with me. I'll fill you in when we get there. Just suffice it to say, your job will be important to someone."

"Who?"

Kujo grinned. "Whoever needs you most."

"That's kind of vague, if you ask me."

"It's the nature of the work," Kujo said.

"Just what exactly does this job entail?" Jake asked.

"Don't worry." Kujo led the way down the stairs of the apartment complex and out to a shiny, black SUV. "I fully intend to brief you on your position and the nature of Hank's organization. But first, I'd like to get out of here and up into the mountains."

Jake climbed into the SUV, silently cursing his prosthetic when it banged against the door. Once in his seat, he buckled his seatbelt, wondering what the hell he was doing and when the hell he'd get that drink Kujo promised. Thankfully, he hadn't committed to anything, which was his only saving grace. What kind of job could Hank have in mind for a one-legged, former Navy SEAL?

ABOUT THE AUTHOR

ELLE JAMES also writing as MYLA JACKSON is a *New York Times* and *USA Today* Bestselling author of books including cowboys, intrigues and paranormal adventures that keep her readers on the edges of their seats. When she's not at her computer, she's traveling, snow skiing, boating, or riding her ATV, dreaming up new stories. Learn more about Elle James at www.ellejames.com

Website | Facebook | Twitter | GoodReads | Newsletter | BookBub | Amazon

Or visit her alter ego Myla Jackson at mylajackson.com
Website | Facebook | Twitter | Newsletter

Follow Me!
www.ellejames.com
ellejames@ellejames.com

ALSO BY ELLE JAMES

Brotherhood Protectors Colorado

SEAL Salvation (#1)

Rocky Mountain Rescue (#2)

Ranger Redemption (#3)

Tactical Takeover (#4)

Shadow Assassin (crossover)

Delta Force Strong

Ivy's Delta (Delta Force 3 Crossover)

Breaking Silence (#1)

Breaking Rules (#2)

Breaking Away (#3)

Breaking Free (#4)

Breaking Hearts (#5)

Iron Horse Legacy

Soldier's Duty (#1)

Ranger's Baby (#2)

Marine's Promise (#3)

SEAL's Vow (#4)

Warrior's Resolve (#5)

Brotherhood Protectors Series

Montana SEAL (#1)

Bride Protector SEAL (#2)

Montana D-Force (#3)

Cowboy D-Force (#4)

Montana Ranger (#5)

Montana Dog Soldier (#6)

Montana SEAL Daddy (#7)

Montana Ranger's Wedding Vow (#8)

Montana SEAL Undercover Daddy (#9)

Cape Cod SEAL Rescue (#10)

Montana SEAL Friendly Fire (#11)

Montana SEAL's Mail-Order Bride (#12)

SEAL Justice (#13)

Ranger Creed (#14)

Delta Force Rescue (#15)

Dog Days of Christmas (#16)

Montana Rescue (Sleeper SEAL)

Hot SEAL Salty Dog (SEALs in Paradise)

Hot SEAL,Hawaiian Nights (SEALs in Paradise)

Hot SEAL Bachelor Party (SEALs in Paradise)

Hot SEAL, Independence Day (SEALs in Paradise)

Brotherhood Protectors Vol 1

The Outrider Series

Homicide at Whiskey Gulch (#1)

Hideout at Whiskey Gulch (#2)

Hellfire Series

Hellfire, Texas (#1)

Justice Burning (#2)

Smoldering Desire (#3)

Hellfire in High Heels (#4)

Playing With Fire (#5)

Up in Flames (#6)

Total Meltdown (#7)

Declan's Defenders

Marine Force Recon (#1)

Show of Force (#2)

Full Force (#3)

Driving Force (#4)

Tactical Force (#5)

Disruptive Force (#6)

Mission: Six

One Intrepid SEAL

Two Dauntless Hearts

Three Courageous Words

Four Relentless Days

Five Ways to Surrender

Six Minutes to Midnight

Hearts & Heroes Series

Wyatt's War (#1)

Mack's Witness (#2)

Ronin's Return (#3)

Sam's Surrender (#4)

Take No Prisoners Series

SEAL's Honor (#1)

SEAL'S Desire (#2)

SEAL's Embrace (#3)

SEAL's Obsession (#4)

SEAL's Proposal (#5)

SEAL's Seduction (#6)

SEAL'S Defiance (#7)

SEAL's Deception (#8)

SEAL's Deliverance (#9)

SEAL's Ultimate Challenge (#10)

Texas Billionaire Club

Tarzan & Janine (#1)

Something To Talk About (#2)

Who's Your Daddy (#3)

Love & War (#4)

Billionaire Online Dating Service

The Billionaire Husband Test (#1)

The Billionaire Cinderella Test (#2)

The Billionaire Bride Test (#3)

The Billionaire Daddy Test (#4)

The Billionaire Matchmaker Test (#5)

The Billionaire Glitch Date (#6)

The Billionaire Perfect Date (#7) coming soon

The Billionaire Replacement Date (#8) coming soon

The Billionaire Wedding Date (#9) coming soon

Ballistic Cowboy

Hot Combat (#1)

Hot Target (#2)

Hot Zone (#3)

Hot Velocity (#4)

Cajun Magic Mystery Series

Voodoo on the Bayou (#1)

Voodoo for Two (#2)

Deja Voodoo (#3)

Cajun Magic Mysteries Books 1-3

SEAL Of My Own

Navy SEAL Survival

Navy SEAL Captive

Navy SEAL To Die For

Navy SEAL Six Pack

Devil's Shroud Series

Deadly Reckoning (#1)

Deadly Engagement (#2)

Deadly Liaisons (#3)

Deadly Allure (#4)

Deadly Obsession (#5)

Deadly Fall (#6)

Covert Cowboys Inc Series

Triggered (#1)

Taking Aim (#2)

Bodyguard Under Fire (#3)

Cowboy Resurrected (#4)

Navy SEAL Justice (#5)

Navy SEAL Newlywed (#6)

High Country Hideout (#7)

Clandestine Christmas (#8)

Thunder Horse Series

Hostage to Thunder Horse (#1)

Thunder Horse Heritage (#2)

Thunder Horse Redemption (#3)

Christmas at Thunder Horse Ranch (#4)

Demon Series

Hot Demon Nights (#1)

Demon's Embrace (#2)

Tempting the Demon (#3)

Lords of the Underworld

Witch's Initiation (#1)

Witch's Seduction (#2)

The Witch's Desire (#3)

Possessing the Witch (#4)

Stealth Operations Specialists (SOS)

Nick of Time

Alaskan Fantasy

Boys Behaving Badly Anthology

Rogues (#1)

Blue Collar (#2)

Pirates (#3)

Stranded (#4)

First Responder (#5)

Blown Away

Warrior's Conquest

Enslaved by the Viking Short Story

Conquests

Smokin' Hot Firemen

Protecting the Colton Bride

Protecting the Colton Bride & Colton's Cowboy Code

Heir to Murder

Secret Service Rescue

High Octane Heroes

Haunted

Engaged with the Boss

Cowboy Brigade

Time Raiders: The Whisper

Bundle of Trouble

Killer Body

Operation XOXO

An Unexpected Clue

Baby Bling

Under Suspicion, With Child

Texas-Size Secrets

Cowboy Sanctuary

Lakota Baby

Dakota Meltdown

Beneath the Texas Moon

Made in the USA
Middletown, DE
11 January 2023

21804887R00141